Adventures
Of
The Angels
By
Lew Duffey

Adventures of the Angels
By Lew Duffey

ISBN#978-0-6151-4159-6

Adventures of the Angels
Introduction

When I started writing this I decided to let my imagination run wild. I hope you will do the same. None of us know what tomorrow will bring. Our concept of God is limited by our ability to expand our mind. None have ever been able to expand their minds far enough to understand the full concept of who, what, where and how God is. I won't pretend that I am any different.

I will take this opportunity to remind you that this is a novel. Keep in mind that many of the stories Jesus told were parables. These were fictitious stories to bring the truth to the level of the people to whom he was talking.

Those people thought the whole world was right where they were. They thought they were living in the center of the universe, whatever they thought that was and that the sun was rising in the east every morning and setting in the west. They gave no thought to the idea that the world was round and it was actually revolving around the sun while at the same time it turned on its own axis.

There are many mysteries that are not yet explained. Probably many of them will not be explained in this lifetime. We will have to wait till we reach the Heavenly shores. So, take this as a novel, but look for truths anywhere you can find them.

It is my hope you will find this book enlightening and at the same time enjoyable. Thank you and May God Bless,

Lew Duffey (Author)

Adventures of the Angels

Chapter 1 (The Trip Begins)

Ten…. Nine…. Eight…. Seven…. Six…. Five…. Four…. We have ignition!   Two….

One…. We have lift-off.

The words rang in Frank's ears. He sat at the controls of the ship, excitement

rolling through his entire body. He would not have control of the ship until it made three

revolutions around the earth. On the third revolution it would be lifted out of the

gravitational pull of the planet. At this point Frank would assume the duties now being

done by the computerized, on-board navigational system.

He would then set his course which would take him to the space station located

just past the planet Mars, where he would board another shuttle which was built entirely

in outer space. That shuttle would become the first segment of a space station just past

the planet, Saturn.

Frank did not know what was going to happen before he ever saw that space

station. For that matter, neither did Arty. As a way of helping Frank relax, Arty struck

up a conversation. Arty was Frank's Guardian Angel. He had come to Frank on a night

when Frank was searching for answers. In spite of all the comforts of the twenty-third

century, Frank had been fighting depression.

He had been taking little comfort in the cars that had no wheels. Vehicles, which defy gravity, gave him little peace of mind. That was when Arty came into his life.

"Remember when we first met?" Arty asked. Frank reflected back to that night in the bar when Arty appeared before him. There were others there that night. They found his appearance to be scary, to say the least. Frank had found him to be a wonderful friend.

"We were soul brothers from the beginning," Frank lamented. Arty did not answer at first. When he finally did answer, he offered a piece of information that Frank did not fully understand.

"I wasn't supposed to be there that night. At least my superior had thought he had made a colossal blunder. But the Master seemed to know why I was there and that's why I came back. You are going to be a servant of the Master and of mankind. You will save the eternal souls of many before you are through."

Frank did not press for more. He simply watched as the onboard computer tallied up the progress of the ship. They were now completing their first revolution and the navigational system was resetting for the second revolution which would climb even higher above the Earth.

He glanced up from the panel and turned to look at Arty but Arty wasn't there. He may be an Angel now, but Arty still had a streak of devil in him.

"Hey, look in front of you," he instructed Frank. Frank followed the voice and found himself looking out of the window of his ship into space. There floating just ahead of him was his old friend.

"I'm just showing off," Arty said with that look of impishness that had so often driven Andora crazy in his life before his resurrection.

"This is fun," he cried in the kind of voice that a little boy used when he first went swimming. Frank watched in amazement.

Meanwhile, back on Earth, Allison and George were among the many who watched, as Frank burst through the third and final orbit of the Earth and into outer space.

There was a loud applause from everyone in the command center, but nobody felt the excitement of the lift-off as much as George and Allison. They, after all, knew more of why Frank was heading into outer space than anyone there. At least, they thought they did. There was something they did not know. Even Arty did not expect it, but it was about to happen.

At this particular instant in all of eternity, there was a call to the Heavenly Hosts. It was a special meeting, called by the Master.

"There will be a slight change in plans," the Master announced. Frank will eventually go to the Space Station Mars, but first we must take him and Arty on a little trip into the past. They are heading for a place where Arty will surely know how to handle a problem which can affect the future of the human race negatively if we do not do some fine tuning."

It was Gabrielle, who spoke first. He wanted to know where they were going and why. The Master simply explained that he would know soon and prepared them for the change in history.

It was at this point that Frank took over the controls of the shuttle. He accelerated to five times the speed they had been traveling and was in the process of readjusting his destination settings when he saw a flash coming from the depths of space.

"What is that?" he cried. The people at the command center heard his cry, but they did not see what he saw. Then they lost him.

"He's vanished," yelled one of the attendants. He got on the radio quickly to ask those who monitored the flight from the other side of the world if they knew anything, but nobody saw anything. Frank and his shuttle simply vanished

"Allison was beside herself, until Andora came to reassure her that this was a planned trip which would end up for the best of all. George was reassured by Harmony, another Angel that this was a controlled situation. They both comforted their charges by telling them that Frank would see them again. More than that, even the two Angels did not know.

Meanwhile, Arty had been briefed on the upcoming trip and was busy prompting Frank to respond without fear.

"I'm here with you and this is going to be the trip of your life," he exclaimed. Frank followed his directions.

When the blinding light was gone, he realized he was headed back to the Earth. Frank's first impulse was to try to turn around, but Arty advised him to land the vehicle. Frank had been trained to do this and he had no reason to question Arty, although he had no idea why he would go back to Earth so quickly.

As he descended toward the Earth he made three revolutions, just as he had on take-off. As he finished the third orbit Arty instructed him to put it down in the desert.

"Desert," Frank repeated but more in the form of a question. He was at a loss for words. There were no deserts in the Twenty-third Century. They had been by then replaced by giant cities that went on forever. Deserts were hot and dry and Frank was used to a world where the entire planet had become air conditioned. Some scientist had discovered how to use the greenhouse effect as a way to completely control the planet's weather. That meant there were no hurricanes, storms, typhoons, twisters no uncontrolled winds of any kind. The way it worked was rather unique. The polar caps had been refrigerated to keep them from melting further. This had become necessary to keep the problem of global warming in check. In the twentieth century there were those who had been afraid that the melting polar caps would cause flooding by raising the sea level and thus wiping out much of the land where people could thrive. This is why Frank was amazed that there was a desert.

"What has happened to the Earth?" he asked. "How did this come on so fast?" As he set the ship down, Arty explained that he was in the past.

"This was the Earth," he began. "The Master has taken us into the past to correct some problem."

"What problem?" pressed Frank. Arty could not tell him because as of this moment he didn't know. It is hard to explain because Frank saw time and Arty saw time from different perspectives. It would actually only be an instant until Arty had the answers, but to Frank it would be several hours.

Arty was not surprised when he found himself standing in the Master's Chambers surrounded by his friends, Gabriel, Andora, Harmony and the Master, himself.

"What's up?" he asked.   The Master began talking as if Arty had not uttered a word.

"We have a Situation," he began. "There is a man living in the same time and in the city where your mortal body met its end, Arty. This man will eventually run for President of the United States, although he will not get far in the Primaries and that is not the reason why you and your space traveler will have to save his life."

Arty listened quietly. He was not sure he really wanted to see that old town ever again, but if the Master asked he knew he would go.

"Andora, you and Harmony will serve as back-up for Arty. Keep yourselves out of sight, but help Arty figure out how to save this mans life. His name is Brian Dunham.

"If he isn't ever going to be president, why do we have to save him?" inquired Arty. He knew who Brian Dunham was. He was the banker Arty had robbed before his death. The Master went into an in depth discussion as to why this mans life meant so much. Although he would never do anything that would have a profound effect on the history of man, he would father a son who would father a son and thus create a person who would be born, live and die before Frank was ever born.

"Out of the seed of the man you are to save will come a man who will help set up the first Solar Shield that protects the Earth during the time in which Frank lives," the Master explained. "This person must live!" Satan would like to destroy him and that is why we must stop him." The Master would not elaborate more. He simply instructed Arty and his helpers on how to stop the death of a man that nobody would have ever thought would have been missed if he were killed.

"By the way, Arty, you will have to instruct Frank to hide that space ship somewhere. It would not be good for people in the old west, where you came from to even know such things exist, yet."

All this took place in the time it took Frank to blink his eyes. By the time he had reopened them Arty had left, been to the meeting and come back again. He explained the situation to Frank who listened with great interest. Then he stared thoughtfully.

"Is time simply another dimension?" he asked. This prompted Arty to explain that this was how the Master was able to know all and see all.

"He is the future, the past and the present!" Arty stated after explaining as best he could. Frank now found himself in a past that was so far removed from anything he knew that he could not identify with his reason for being there.

"But, why is the Master sending me?" he pressed. "I realize that you are more than human, now. I am still a man. Why is he sending me?"

Arty did not know the reason for this, yet. He was sure, however, that the Master would tell him when the time was right, possibly the next time Frank blinked an eye.

"Let's just set this baby down now," he instructed. "Consider this an experience that none of your friends have ever experienced. Try to find a place where we can hide it. People in the old west would surely get spooked if they found one of those things setting in the desert.

As Arty prompted him, Frank maneuvered the ship into its orbital path and finally set it down in the southwestern part of the United States.

Frank looked around him. He knew there would be big shopping malls and high-rise housing projects everywhere in the century Twenty-Three-thousand and twenty three. He would get his first taste of what the Earth would be like without climate control when he finally stepped outside the shuttle.

Chapter 2 (Tradesman County)

Once the ship was on the ground Frank tried to open the hatch, but it would not open. Arty prompted him to wait.

"I think you are going to have to let it cool down. It's not supposed to, but it seems the door has swollen more than the hull of the ship. Until it cools, just relax and we will try to consider why we are here."

"Why do you suppose it's jammed?" asked Frank. Arty explained that the Earth was not climate-controlled at this point in history and the reason was most likely humidity and excessive heat—two of the conditions the great, great grandson of the man they were supposed to save would eventually create to save the planet Earth.

Frank listened as Arty related all the facts he had learned in the meeting with the Master. He was careful to point out that although Brian Dunham was not one who would make any great advances for civilization, there would be someone born of his seed that was a crucial part of the Master's plan for man's salvation. He mentioned that someone who would remind him very much of Mordrid—the one who had tried to hold Arty's spirit captive for eternity—was working for Satan.

"Satan will try anything he can to upset the Master's long range plans," Arty stated with great emphasis. Even Arty did not know of the surprise which would await him when he finally met up with this demon.

Eventually the door was opened and Frank stepped out of the ship. He was amazed that the air he breathed did not seem to irritate his throat. It seemed to smell of a fragrance he had never experienced before. There were no pollutants, no carbon monoxide and the sky was blue with the most beautiful white fluffy clouds he had ever seen.

"Wow," he said. "Are we really on the Earth?" Arty smiled.

"Yeah," he answered. "I had forgotten how great it was. I wish now, I would have taken the time to appreciate it more when I was a man. Let's find a place to hide this ship."

They found an old deserted farm not far from where they touched down and as Arty instructed, Frank taxied the ship into the old barn.   They got another break, too. The old farm was deserted because the owner had been a bank robber and was shot during an attempted robbery of the Tradesman County Bank. He never made it as far as Arty had.

Arty instructed Frank to put on the clothes he found in the farmhouse, including the side shooter. Frank mentioned that he could never shoot anyone, but Arty reassured him that he would not have to.

You do have to look like you would, though," Arty said. "I want to take you outside and let you practice using that thing. They spent the next several hours with Arty instructing and Frank practicing with the gun. At first he was not coming close to the target that Arty had him set up to practice on, but after many attempts, he was starting to hit the target more often than he missed.

"You're doing great," Arty praised. "Now practice your draw." Frank blinked.

"My draw?" Frank repeated in the form of question. Arty had donned his old cowboy clothes, complete with side arm and with his levitation abilities he showed Frank how it was done.

"I could never shoot anyone," Frank repeated again, but Arty reassured him that he would not have to.

"You just need to make them think you would if you had to," he explained again.

The two started in the direction of the town. As they walked into the town, Arty saw the old wood shed where Andora had waited for him the day he robbed the bank.

"I robbed that bank," he told Frank bluntly as he pointed to the Tradesman County Bank.

"Andora and I would have gotten away if the wagon hadn't gone over a cliff with us in it. You know," he went on, "They never did find the money we stole. I reckon it sunk to the bottom of the river."

Arty grew silent for a moment when he realized he was starting to pick up that 'Arty' accent again.

"Huh!" he uttered to himself. Then he pulled himself out of his reverie and put his mind back on the business at hand.

"We need to find out where Brian Dunham is. Then, we need to find out what kind of danger he is in." Even as he spoke, Arty realized that he knew where he would find Dunham. He was always at the bank until closing time. Still, he needed to know the danger and how they could stop the threat.

Just as Frank did, Arty had wondered why the Master wanted Frank to come on this trip. It would have been so much easier for him if he were alone or working with Andora or Harmony. They could travel from point to point in a split second and even move back and forth through time as needed, but Frank, being human, could only run on what the Angels called Reel-time.

One of those instantaneous trips was about to occur again. In the time it took for Frank to blink, Arty was called to the Master for another meeting. Arty, Andora and Harmony were briefed on the upcoming project. They were told just how they were to go about saving the life of the banker he had robbed the day before his Earthly death occurred.

Arty could read the smile on Andorra's face. It was that smug look she always wore when she was right about something and he was usually the one to whom she was saying, "I told you so." Somehow it did not infuriate him so much now as it did in the old days. Arty had to admit that this was a strange turn of events. Maybe it was the Master's way of freeing him from the guilt of having threatened the life of the banker. The more Arty thought about it, the more he became certain that this was, indeed the Master's way of giving him the chance to pay for his human failures.

Andora had realized this from the very beginning.

As Frank opened his eyes, Arty was back and began to explain what the Master had wanted. He explained that Frank was brought back with him into his own past because Arty would be at a disadvantage to try to work with the people there. The reason was quite simple. They would see Arty as a ghost and be scared of him.

In truth there was more. The Master was preparing Frank for experiences that no man had ever experienced before. It was for Frank's growth as much as anything else, but the Master did not feel this was the time to share that information with Arty.

Frank had to train to be a cowboy and Arty would work through him. Arty was rather proud of himself. He had already taken care of that part. The Master had been quick to praise him on his quick thinking.

Frank was beginning to get used to the fact that a lot of things seemed to be changing in an instant, so he simply listened as they walked.

Arty noticed a horse standing in the field near the old wood shed. Upon closer inspection he found no brand. This horse evidently did not belong to anyone. So he instructed Frank to move closer with some hay in hand. Then Arty noticed an old rope and instructed Frank on how to tie it into a noose.

"I want you to bridle that horse. You will need transportation and he does not seem to have an owner. It may as well be you," he prompted.

After several attempts, Frank was able to bridle the horse. Arty told him he would have to ride bareback for now. There was no saddle to be found. The first time Frank swung himself onto the horse's back the horse bolted and threw him to the ground.

The Stallion took off across country. Frank found himself lying on the ground, dusty and sore. He thought at first that he had broken a bone or two.

Arty reassured himself that Frank was alright and went off to run down the horse. The stallion was sure spooked when Arty stood directly in front of him and when he turned away, Arty simply reappeared there. As a cowboy, Arty had been good with horses and it paid off now.

After some time and in a voice slightly above a whisper, he soon had her walking with him back to Frank.

Frank was amazed to hear his voice coming from Arty's lips. The reason was soon explained. The horse would be used to Frank's voice and would thereby take to him as she had Arty.

"We'll call her 'Babe,' " Arty said with that old rye grin that was the old Arty's favorite smile.

They spent the better part of the afternoon breaking the horse, as Arty put it. Then Frank began to feel hungry.

"I can help with that," Arty offered. "You'll have to get used eating like I did. It may take some adjusting, but I think you'll learn to enjoy it."

Arty showed him food that grew in the wild. At first Frank did not care for the taste of some of it, but eventually he learned to like foods like dandelion, wild flowers. Arty showed him which ones to pick. Frank found that Queen Anne's lace tasted similar to carrots. He also tried the leaves of the Prickly Ash tree. It also had tasty berries on it. Arty showed him where wild blackberries could be found.

Something that Frank had not thought to bring along with him from the ship was his supplement tablets. That was just as well because he would not need them here. In the twenty-third century everyone took these supplements because they had the same amount of antioxidant vitamins in them as the fruits and vegetables no longer grown. Years of pollution had drained the earth of much of its life-giving properties, so man had to create an alternate source of these vitamins and minerals. Otherwise, there would be even more heart patients than there already were.

What Frank was not thinking about as he ate was the fact that for the first time in his life he did not need supplements. These plants still offered everything his body would need. He tried wild blackberries and Autumn Olive Berries which contain seventeen times more lycopen, ounce for ounce, than tomatoes did, even in the twentieth century, let alone the twenty-third century. Frank found himself breathing easier, too. The air was pure and dry.

When they got to town, the two headed for the bank. Frank walked up to Dunham and greeted him. Mr. Dunham seemed a little sheepish as he welcomed the stranger. He was still a little nervous after the experience he had with Arty. That robbery had only been a week before. Arty knew why Dunham was nervous and prompted Frank to simply explain that he was considering opening an account and wanted more information about the bank.

"There's only been two attempts to rob this bank," Mr. Dunham said. One of them got shot by yours truly. The other guy and his girls are lying in a pauper's grave over at the cemetery. He got away with a bundle, but he couldn't outrun the posse."

Arty might have been angry at the sound of Dunham's voice as he spoke in the past, but now he was above that.

"I'm new in town," Frank offered. "Where is there a good place to bed down?" Dunham told him there was a hotel down the street which would not be hard to find. There was only one street in this town. The cost was fifty cents a night. This came as a shock to Frank. It wasn't really information he could use, though. He had no money.

Arty realized that he wouldn't get far unless he had some money. He prompted Frank to ask if anyone in town needed hired help. Dunham sent him to the Tradesman Stable.

Soon Frank had a job paying seventy-five cents a day plus room and board. Now Arty knew he could concentrate on how to protect Mr. Dunham from the would-be killer.

It turned out that it was another bank robbery attempt. This time the man who would rob the bank would not be as kind as Arty had been. Arty had to find out who this was and when and how it was to come down.

Frank had worked hard his first day and was completely exhausted. He was soon asleep. Arty was called for another conference.

Arty found himself, Andora and Harmony standing in front of the Master. He was about ready to ask 'what now?' but the Master spoke first.

"I am going to take you on a speed trip through time," he announced. "It is important that you understand the mind of the man who is going to try to rob the same bank you did, Arty. The difference is this. You were in control so you did not resort to violence. This man is not a professional. He will panic and then wish he had not done it for the rest of his short life unless you stop him. You must not resort to violence. The man is a good man, but his life has taken him in the wrong direction. His wife and kids were just lost in a fire and he has given up hope. He will do what he does out of this sense of hopelessness. Arty, Andora and Harmony, your job is to restore his hope. If not, this is what will happen."

As he said this, they found themselves standing in the Tradesman County Bank while Mr. Dunham prepared to close up. A tall, thin blond-haired man with a bandana over his face forced his way into the bank with a pistol and demanded the banker to give him all the money in the safe.

Dunham was still nervous over the robbery he had just lived through with Arty. He had purchased a rifle. It was with that rifle that he killed the next bank robber. Not being much of a gunslinger, the gun did not help him much. He was lucky when the robber came in, but this time he would fumble for the rifle. The man reached for it and the two struggled for its possession. During the scuffle the bandana fell from the man's face. Dunham saw the fear as he realized that now he could easily be identified. He raised his pistol and fired into the heart of the banker.

As soon as he realized what he had done he staggered backward and stared at the lifeless figure on the floor. Arty could read his mind and knew just what he was thinking. They were thoughts of panic. He never even tried to get the money, he simply started to run. In his panic, he never gave a thought to his horse.

Cowboys who heard the shot came running from the saloon. The first man to get to the bank went in and saw Mr. Dunham on the floor. He came running out yelling.

"That guy," he yelled as he looked at the tall cowboy running down the street. "He killed Dunham." Guns started firing and it ended with the tall stranger lying on the street, face down with his gun in his hand and Dunham inside the bank, dead.

The Master charged Arty, Andora and Harmony with saving both lives. That is to say, he wanted them to save the life of Dunham and the life of Henry Haskins. The plan was that they visit the man and find out what he was thinking and work at replacing the hopelessness with a faith that would save both lives.

While Frank slept, Arty, Andora and Harmony now found themselves in the desert as the form of another sleeping man lay close to his horse and a fire which was almost burned out lay before them.

Arty and Andora were happy that they finally were able to work together. The fact that they were in Tradesman County caused them both to become rather reminiscent.

"Honey, I'm home," exclaimed Arty with that impish sound in his voice that had so many times caused Andorra's heart to melt.

"Okay, Mr. smart guy," she said with an impish voice of her own. "What do we do now?"

Harmony had been watching with amusement until now. When it became apparent to her that Arty had no idea of what to do next, she took command.

"Let's delve into this man's mind while he sleeps," she offered. "We need to know what hurt he is not dealing with very well and help him.

"How do we start?" asked Arty. He listened as Harmony started to open up the mind of the sleeping man before them.

"Concentrate on him," instructed Harmony. "Dig within your own mind and tune it into his."

The three Angels tuned into the mind of the cowboy and saw a young Henry Haskins working in a vegetable garden.

Chapter 3 (The Past of Henry Haskins)

It was a beautiful day. The sun was just beginning to set in the west. Huge fluffy white clouds floated peacefully across the sky, driven only by the slight breeze from the west. It gave the appearance that they were traveling away from the sun as if they were trying to recapture the afternoon, thus avoiding the end of the day.

The breeze cooled the farmer as he worked. Henry heard a familiar voice calling to him. His wife was calling him to dinner.

Henry pulled his hanky out of his pocket and wiped the sweat from his forehead.

"I'll be there in about fifteen minutes," he called back to her. I still have to till about ten feet of soil, yet. Sundown will be here soon and I don't want to leave this undone.

Henry went back to work. While he worked his mind was a maze of activity for Arty, Harmony and Andora to travel through.

His wife had strawberry-colored hair. There were a few freckles. Just enough freckles to add to her beauty. She had brown eyes and a perky little nose that Henry loved to tweak. He would usually cause her to respond by grabbing him in his ribs making him laugh, and many times this led to a lovemaking session.

They had Josh, but Henry and Dot both wanted more children. Henry hoped the next one would be a girl. Dot didn't care much.

"Just so it has ten fingers and ten toes," she would say. "If it's healthy I will thank God above. I will love whatever he sends us.

The three Angels watched the 'instant replay' of his memories with great interest. Arty knew how Henry felt about this woman. He had felt the same way about Andora. He only wished he had shown her more love while they were flesh and blood.

Andora sent him a reminder that he had given her more love than he ever knew. Harmony interrupted the personal conversation and called them back to the task of Henry Haskins.

"While the farmer worked, his mind took him back to the day he met Dot. He was in town picking up supplies for his father who had owned the farm he now owned until his father died about twelve years ago.

"Is that twelve years ago our time, or seven years ago at the point this memory originated?" Arty asked.

"It doesn't matter," said Harmony. Let's just watch and listen. Arty turned his attention back to the memory of Henry Haskins.

As a young Henry entered the general store, he noticed a young girl with red hair, brown eyes and freckles smiling at him. Women did not usually work in general stores. In fact at that point in history they usually didn't work outside the home. That would exclude the bar girls, of course. This young girl was the daughter of the store owner James Wilhide. To say the least, Henry was smitten. He went about collecting the items his father had sent him for and took them to the cash register where Dot stood smiling. She added up the cost on an old pad and gave them to him along with a handwritten receipt. Henry wanted to ask her out, but he was to shy so he simply picked up the items and walked out. He found himself volunteering to go for supplies before his father even asked, just for the pleasure of seeing her again.

One day while he was shopping two men came into the store. They did not see Henry because he was behind some shelves in the back of the store searching for a shovel to replace the one his father had broken while digging some roots out of his garden.

"Hey sweetheart," said one of the men. "What's a sweet thing like you doin' in a place like this?" He turned and winked to his friend who picked up on the conversation.

"Yeah," he added. "You should be workin' over at the saloon. A beautiful girl like you could get a guy turned on pretty good."

"Are you here to buy something?" Dot answered. "If not, there's the door. Don't let it hit you on the way out."

Henry stretched to look around the shelf. He saw the man climb around the counter that stood between him and the frightened girl and try to capture her in his arms. She quickly moved aside causing him to trip and fall. His friend reached for the girl and grabbed her roughly.

"Let's not be unfriendly," he chided. "All we want is a little love." He cried out in pain when she grabbed him right where he wanted to be grabbed, but not in such an ungentle way.

"You little bitch," he howled. "I'll teach you to respect a gentleman. Dot smacked him across the face. If he did have her she would surely make him pay.

"You are no gentleman," she countered.

That was when Henry came running around the shelf, grabbed the fool by the arm. He spun him around and hit him hard right below the belt. The man doubled over in pain. The other man was just getting up from his fall and made an attempt at revenging his friend, but Henry was young and strong. After all, he had tilled acres of farmland with a plow that was made for a man to push. His father could not afford a horse.

Henry stepped aside, grabbed the man's arm and twisted it. This caused the man to fall again. Still cursing, the idiot tried to get up, but Henry put his foot down on the man's fingers and pressed.

"Those boots could fix ya so you would never use a six shooter again," he chided. "Do you want me to show you how it's done?"

The man looked up at him with fear in his eyes. When his friend got up, Henry looked at him menacingly. The man simply backed away and ran out the door. Henry looked back at the man whose fingers he was stepping on.

"Do you want to leave while you can still use your hand?" he asked. The man shook his head and Henry took his boot off the fool's fingers and pulled him to his feet, literally throwing him toward the door.

"Get out of here," he shouted. "If I ever hear that you bothered this lady again I will break your fingers."

Arty was acting more and more like the old gunslinger he had been in life. He was rooting young Henry on with great passion. Andora was taken with the memory this had created in her. It brought to life memories of the rootin' tootin' cowboy that Arty had been. She remembered always feeling comfortable when she was with Arty because, as she used to say,

"If anyone ever bothered me, Arty would saw his toes off." Her audience laughed. Both Harmony and Arty brought Andora out of her reverie with their laughter.

"Well, it's true," she said emphatically. Then they all turned their attention to the action which was being replayed in Henry's dream state.

Dot stood a little shakily, but she managed to pull herself together enough to thank this kind young man.

"What's your name?" asked Henry. Dot introduced herself and a love affair began.

It was not more than six months later that they got married. They moved into the old bunkhouse on his father's farm. Henry worked with his father and Dot, who left the store, worked with Henry's mother, keeping house.

That was when things turned bad for Henry. Seymour Raven, who owned a large spread next to Mr. Haskins farm, decided he wanted to expand. He approached Henry's dad about buying, but Mr. Haskins was not interested in selling.

Over the next six to eight months Henry noticed that some of the livestock was missing. He had a bad feeling about this so he slept out at the edge of the woods on the east side of the farm to keep an eye for whoever it was that was rustlin' cattle.

Eventually, he dozed off only to be awakened by the sound of gunshots and loud screaming. Henry jumped to his feet. What he saw was the farmhouse and stable burning.

"Oh, God!" he gasped. "Oh God, I have to help them. I have to help them."

He was yelling for Dot as he ran across the field toward the house. A group of men went riding off toward the west. They didn't hear him yelling. When Henry saw them he stopped yelling. He pulled out his rifle and aimed at one of the riders. Henry winged him in the shoulder, causing the man to fall from his horse.

Then he turned his attention back to the farmhouse. His heart sank when he realized that the old bunkhouse was aflame too. His wife and newborn baby as well as his mother and father could never have lived through this. The fire had made it impossible to get close to either of the burning buildings.

Henry ran back to where the man he had just shot lay. He wasn't in a mood to be gentle and at this point he did not care if the man lived or died. He simply wanted to know who was responsible for this atrocity. Henry grabbed the man by the scruff of the neck.

"Why did you do this?" he practically yelled. "Was it Raven? Was it Raven, who paid you to do this?"

"Yes," the man breathed. "Your father should have sold out." With that his face went blank.

Henry knew Raven's men would come looking for him when they realized that he had shot this man. He jumped on his horse and headed for the hills. As he rode he tried to compose himself. One thing he could not do was forgive Raven. He knew he would make him pay.

It was several days later that he rode into Raven's spread at night. Everyone was asleep when he crept behind the bunkhouse. Inside were the dozen or so cowboys who had done the horrible deed to his family. Now it would be his chance to avenge their deaths.

Henry quietly crept into the barn and got a bail of hay which he carried to the back of the bunkhouse. He then spread the hay under the back window. He carefully opened the window making a brail of hay stacked up the side of the window onto the window ledge.

Once he had done this, he found two pieces of granite. After several attempts he sparked a fire and it did not take long for the fire to quickly spread.

Henry took his rifle and waited in the front of the bunkhouse. Before long, the place was on fire. Henry heard voices inside, and as the first figure came running out the front door, he shot. Then the second man, and then the third, were shot as they ran out. Some of them never got out before they were overcome with smoke.

Henry saw lamps being lit in the main house. He found a place to hide by the well and watched as Seymour Raven came running out with a rifle in hand. Henry never gave him a chance. He aimed and squeezed the trigger and Raven fell to the ground.

Mrs. Raven was right beside him as he fell. Henry aimed at her, but could not bring himself to fire. Instead, he mounted up and rode away.

Now Henry knew there would be a bounty on his head. He knew that he had to find a place to hide, so he rode all night long and halfway through the next day before he had to stop and rest.

He found an empty house which he figured was about at the edge of Raven's land. It had been used by one of the farmers who had sold out and moved. Once Henry was sure there was nobody there, he went inside and lay on the bed. He was soon sound asleep.

It was only then that Arty dared to talk. He turned his attention from the sleeping man and turned toward Harmony.

"Why didn't we come back to keep his family from being killed?" he asked in a whisper.

"You don't have to whisper," said Harmony. "Remember, he can't hear us unless we want him to. Besides, this is like an instant replay. The Master has reviewed it. If it would not have changed the course of history for so many people in a negative way, he surely would have changed it. Remember the scripture, 'All things work for the good of those who love the Lord.' Nobody said all things would be good!"

Arty nodded and Harmony told him they should keep watching. That's what they did.

The next morning Henry awoke. The first thing he thought about was his wife and child. He was trying to adjust to the fact that he would never see them again. Somehow, he didn't want to live without them. The next thing he thought about was what he had done a day and a half ago. He was not too happy that he had decided to take the law into his own hands. Now, he was filled with remorse, but nothing could change what had happened to him and what he did to those men.

Henry was hungry and there was no food in the old ranch house. He picked up his rifle and went hunting jackrabbits. It did not take long before he kicked one up, built a fire to cook it and then sat down to eat.

"I'm gonna need money," he thought to himself. I'm gonna need to get as far away from here as I can." He knew he wasn't more than a half day ride from the Tradesman County Bank. Henry finished eating, got on his horse and rode.

When he got to the edge of town Henry was careful not to be seen. He hitched his horse behind the saloon and crept between it and the building next to it. He took his bandana and made a mask which he tied around his neck. When nobody was within eyesight he quickly maneuvered around the corner and literally burst into the bank, eyes blazing with a mixture of grief and fear as well as anger.

"Give me as much money as you can fit in these saddlebags," he barked as he threw them at the banker. That was when the banker tried to get his rifle and Henry shot him.

Arty looked from the scene to Andora and Harmony. He remembered his days as an outlaw. He had shot many people while robbing the many banks that he had knocked off.

"Will he go to Hell for this?" he asked. Harmony smiled, but it was Andora who spoke up next.

"You didn't," she began. "You found your way here. We can only pray that the Master knows this man's heart. We must hope for his eternal salvation, even if his life on Earth is a short one." That was when Harmony spoke.

"Who said it would be a short one?" she asked. "We have to keep him from killing the banker. The rest we let up to the Master."

Now the Angels found themselves standing before the Master once again.

Chapter 4 (The Debriefing)

"Arty," the Master stated emphatically, "Don't concern yourself for the spirit of the living. I am working through all things for the common good of all those who were chosen before their very Birth to become part of my Kingdom."

Arty's surprise was apparent. It was almost as if he still had a physical body with a mouth that dropped open in utter surprise.

"You mean I was preordained to be one of yours?" he questioned. "You mean, you let me do all those terrible things and still knew I would be an Angel?"

"I knew what you did and why you did them," the Master explained. "I also knew that the world you were born into would be full of sin and perils. I can't save the physical lives of all the people, but I can save the spirit of those who I see to be worthy. Now as for the man you are so worried about. Let his eternity be in my hands. You stick with the task at hand. Don't let him change my time line by cutting off the life of one who will be the forefather of a very important part of the future."

Arty was beginning to understand that there was much more to life than survival. One could live to be a ripe old age and still never 'grow up' and therefore never become part of the Heavenly host.

"I'm sorry I questioned you, Sir," Arty offered. Andora and Harmony had stood quietly, listening. Now Andora spoke up.

"We need a plan," she said. The Master told her that this was up to the three of them and Frank. With that, they found themselves standing over the sleeping form of Frank.

Frank continued to work till he had saved some money and while he spent his days working and his nights sleeping, the three Angels were busy working on a plan to stop the death of Dunham.

The plan they finally agreed upon was a non-violent solution. They would distract Henry so he would not load the weapon. This would have meant that Dunham would have been able to grab his shot gun and since they did not want to cause the death of anyone, they had to make sure that Dunham would not have a loaded weapon, either.

As far as Henry was concerned, it would be easy to create the oversight on his part, but they knew they would have to enlist Frank's help with Dunham. He would have to sneak into the bank when it was closed, unload the gun and put it back where he found it. At this point in history there were no such things as burglar alarm systems, monitoring cameras or any kind of security devices, so if all Frank did was take out the bullets and tamper with nothing else, Dunham would be none the wiser.

"We will have to make sure that Dunham does not discover the gun to be empty," Arty cautioned. "One of us will have to stay with him and watch the whole time. Andy, you take that responsibility. Harmony, why don't you simply watch over us all and make sure we don't slip up anywhere. I will tell Frank what he needs to do. I found the lock on the back door is easy to tamper with. I will walk him through it." Then he sort of smiled as he noted, "You know, if I had only looked before I tried to knock off the bank, I could have gotten away without ever being caught."

"One problem," corrected Andora. "You did not have the combination to the safe."

"Oh, yeah!" breathed Arty. "I plumb forgot about that."

Andora took command at this point. The plan Arty had thought up was good as far as it went. They still needed the combination.

"I'll catch Dunham as he opens the bank in the morning and watch him dial the combination. Then we will know what to tell Frank. That way, he can open the safe. We already know that Dunham locks the gun in the safe when he closes up at night. That is why we need to open the safe, take the gun, and take the bullets out of it."

Chapter 5 (The Plan of Action)

While Frank was at work, Andora followed Dunham as he closed up the bank. She watched as he dialed the combination and prepared to take the information to Arty, who would pass it on to Frank.

While she was doing that, Arty decided to check out a favorite hide-out he had used many times when he was a bank robber. It was a cave about a quarter of a mile outside of town. Arty entered the cave and reflected on his life before he became part of the spirit world. His reflection was cut short, though by the appearance of a dark sinister looking being who Arty took to be Mordrid, the demon he and the others had defeated in the twentieth Century.

"Mordrid?" he asked.

"My name is Omar," the demon announced. "I am here to make sure Henry Haskins fulfills our plans for him. He will die, but not before he kills Mr. Dunham."

"Well," exclaimed Arty. "I'm here to spoil your little plan."

Somehow Arty was not scared. In fact, he was more like the old gunslinger he had been in his previous life. If someone challenged him, he would prepare to make them pay.

"You will fail," threatened Omar.

"Oh, is that so," Arty said, but it was more a statement than a question. "We'll see about that."

He had no sooner said that, than the demon disappeared in a burst of smoke. Arty was congratulating himself. He had scared many cowboys with his attitude, causing them to back down from a fight. He thought this demon was smart enough not to want to mess with the man. Then he began to wonder why Omar made himself known.

Arty rejoined the others and told them about the encounter. Harmony explained that Omar had no choice but to make his presence known to anyone who served the Master.

"You see," she began. "The Master allows them to exist for only one reason. They tempt the living. Those who resist their temptations are most worthy of the Kingdom. What I mean is they serve a purpose to the good of those who love the Lord. He would have otherwise destroyed these demons centuries ago. If Omar did not declare himself to us, he would have been cast into Outer Darkness along with Mordrid.

"Man," Arty exclaimed. "That guy sure looked like Mordrid." Harmony explained that they all looked like Mordrid.

"You will get used to it, Arty," she comforted. "Now we have to be extra careful. He knows our plan. He will sneak into the bank and undo our work.

"You mean reload the gun," Arty confirmed. Harmony nodded. This meant they would have to have a backup plan.

Suddenly, it occurred to Arty that they had made this too complicated. He turned to Harmony and asked why they were using Frank for this.

"After all," he began, "we can levitate. That's how Omar will reload the gun, right?"

Harmony looked a little perplexed at first, but then looked at Arty and then toward Andora.

"You know something?" she asked, "Arty has a good point. I wonder why I didn't think of it. Frank can help by getting to know Henry better. You know what I mean? He can listen and encourage the poor man to think of what he is doing. He may even be able to stop him from trying this fool stunt. That would save both lives."

"I think we need to make him reassure himself that his life is worth living," Andora added. Arty, you need to prompt Frank to help this man. He needs to give him the feeling that he is not alone. In truth, he isn't, but right now he doesn't know that. Frank needs to be a friend. You do that and we will make sure that Omar doesn't do anything underhanded to change our plans."

When Frank left his job that evening Arty came to him and explained their plans. He went into great detail to explain that they would not only save the life of Dunham, but also the life of Henry Haskins.

"He needs a friend," Arty began. "He needs someone who will listen to him and I think maybe we can share my life's story with him. That should make him think twice before even trying to rob the bank. If that doesn't work, my friends are standing by with a back-up plan."

Frank was more or less led to the place Arty knew Henry was hiding out. As he stepped around the bush, Henry saw him and tried clumsily to pull his gun. Arty had one hand on Henry and one on Frank. He was pulling positive energy from the universe to give a sense of peace to each man. However, Henry was still a little leery.

"What do you want?" he enquired as his hand rested on the gun which was still in his holster.

"I'm a friend," Frank announced.

"I don't know you," countered Henry.

"No, you don't," answered Frank. "But I know you. I know what happened to you and I know that you need someone right now. You are about to make a serious mistake. If you try robbing that bank, it won't go well for you."

"How did you know about that?" Henry asked incredulously. The shocked look on his face was one of almost panic.

"I know about what happened to your family," Frank began. He was repeating every thought Arty was sending into his mind. Frank went through the whole ordeal. Henry listened with eyes wide with fright and then he began to cry.

"I couldn't help them," he cried out. I couldn't do anything to stop it. All I could think of was how to avenge their death.

"In the same situation, I probably would have done the same," Frank offered. "But, if you try to rob the bank it will only lead to more heartache.

It was then that Omar realized that he was losing control of what he thought was a perfect situation. He had to distract Frank and Henry before Frank could make him realize where he was heading. He created the sound of a gunshot in the woods causing Henry to draw his gun and fire in the direction he thought the shot was coming from.

Arty knew he needed to do something. He made himself visible to the two men and stepped from behind a tree with his gun in his hand. Arty was looking off into the woods with a look of disappointment.

"Dang," he swore. "I think I missed him." Then he looked at Henry and decided he would have to play the part so he looked at Henry's gun and said,

"Hey, man. I was trying to shoot a squirrel. Why don't ya put that gun away?" As he said that he holstered his gun. Henry reluctantly put his gun away.

"Who are you?" he asked. Arty was thinking fast; he knew if he told him his name it would possibly be recognized, so he made up one.

"Arnold Swartzbaugh," he introduced himself. "Folks call me a drifter. I jest live off the land and any odd jobs people will pay me to do. Where are you headed?"

"Tradesman City," said Henry. "I have some business there." Then he looked back at Frank and amended his statement.

"I mean I was headed that way." Arty enquired why he was going and Henry repeated the whole story again.

"Buddy," Arty began. "You don't want to go knockin' off banks. You especially don't want to try the Tradesman County Bank. The last two guys who tried that ended up in the town cemetery. Life ain't easy in the old west, but you can put your life back together if you try. Who knows, you may even find someone else to love once you get over the fear of being hurt again. But pullin' a bank robbery is foolhardy."

Omar was not going to give up so easily but as he stood in the shadows watching Arty, Frank and Henry, he did not know how to distract Henry from the conversation. If he tried the gun routine again, Henry would probably be inclined to think it was just another hunter. He knew he needed something drastic, but he also knew who Arty was and that would make his job harder.

Arty knew his weaknesses, too. That scared him. Therefore, he sat in the shadows and waited for an opportunity. Just what that would be, he didn't know.

Meanwhile, Arty was busy multitasking. He was trying to put on a show for Henry and at the same time, consider what to do about Omar.

"I think I'm going to need help," he thought to himself. Arty summons Harmony and Andora. They stood there in the shadows, unseen by the living as Arty went about being the cowboy that he had been in his life on earth and at the same time asked them what they would do about the situation.

"It's your call," answered Harmony. "I think you know what Omar fears most. Arty's eyes lit up.

"The Bible," he declared. "If I can get him to try to desecrate the scriptures, he will be in violation of the edict. I just have to think of a way to get him to do that."

As the others watched silently, Arty continued his conversation with Henry. He took on the persona of the cowboy he had been in his former life as he spoke.

"You know what happened to one guy who tried to knock off that bank?" he asked. He continued without waiting for an answer.

"He and his girl friend were trying to outrun the posse when the wagon they were in went over a cliff. They ended up at the bottom of a ravine floating in the water. When they fished them out of the water, they just buried them without ceremony and everyone in the town applauded the sheriff. It was a fool thing to try anyway."

Arty didn't tell Henry how many times he had robbed banks before he finally got caught. He wanted to make him think of the negative consequences of what he was considering. It was working, too.

Henry was wondering what he could have been thinking of. He surely was not going to bring his family back and he would be adding insult to their memory by making himself a criminal. It did not occur to him that when he took the life of the rancher and his men; he had already done that. Arty was not going to tell him.

Then it occurred to Arty that he knew a way to get Omar out of the picture before he could tempt Henry into reconsidering. He knew that Henry carried a Bible in his saddlebag. The Bible had belonged to his wife. She had given it to him as an anniversary gift and he had kept it in his saddlebag ever since. It was the only thing left for him to cherish. Henry had not even opened it to read since her death. This gave Arty an idea. Harmony and Andora applauded. Frank wasn't sure what was going on, but he had the feeling that Arty somehow had things under control so he simply watched.

"Hey, man," he began. "You got a Bible?" Henry said that he did and Arty asked if he might see it.

"I was thinkin' about a scripture I wanted to memorize. It starts like, 'the Lord is my shepherd, I shall not want'."

"The 23rd. Psalm—my wife's favorite passage," Henry offered. He went to a tree stump, where he had left the saddle by the horse and pulled the Bible out of his saddlebags and they sat together while he read the 23rd. Psalms and then they talked about other parts of the Bible. This worked. Omar backed further into the shadows. He was not going near that book.

After a while, Henry fell asleep on the ground and Frank lay, looking at the sky. He was curious.

"How do you know about that guy who tried to rob the bank?" Frank asked. Arty explained that the guy was none other then himself. Harmony hushed him, warning him not to say more, but it was already too late. Omar heard and his eyes lit up. He could not imagine why he had not recognized Arty as the cowboy who had robbed that bank before. When he met Arty in that cave he saw an angel but he had no idea of Arty's past until now.

Chapter 6 (Arty's Goof)

"You must watch what you tell the living," Harmony scolded. Omar cannot hear what we say to each other, but he can hear what we tell the living He especially had no trouble hearing you this time because you had made yourself available for the living to see. He is surely on his way to find Mordrid, now."

"But Mordrid is in outer darkness," Arty blurted. As soon as he said that, he realized that Mordrid would not be cast into outer darkness for at least a hundred and fifty years.

"Here's the problem," Harmony began. "We can't force Mordrid into outer darkness until the time when we freed you from slavery to Satan. If we do, we will undo much of history and throw the world into turmoil."

"What can I do?" asked Arty. Harmony answered that he needed to stay with Frank and Henry.

"I must deal with this myself," she exclaimed. Harmony didn't know how she was going to go about this, but she knew she would have to figure something. She was then called before the Master.

"Arty goofed again," said the Master. "Not to worry. I know you can outsmart Omar and Mordrid. Follow them and keep me informed of their every move. You need to make sure the lamp is not destroyed. If it is, Arty and Andora will be destroyed with it."

"But what does the lamp have to do with this, questioned Harmony? It occurred to her, before the Master replied, that Mordrid, knowing that Arty who would lead to his downfall would have to never find his way into the twentieth century.

The Master echoed the thoughts even as she was thinking them. What he did not tell even Harmony was that all of this was a part of his plan.

Harmony focused on her next move. She knew the Master was right. Her next move depended upon what Mordrid and Omar did. She concentrated on finding the two. Sure enough, they were standing in the shadows as she snuck in to spy on them. Mordrid was listening, as Omar told him what Arty had said to Frank.

"But that can't be," exclaimed Mordrid. "Those two are in the lamp and will not be awakened until the twentieth century." Then he turned to Omar. If only he could travel back to the time Arty robbed the bank, he could cause his death and thereby circumvent the damage.

"We can't travel through time backwards," corrected Omar. "Only the Angels have that power. We need to find a way to make sure that lamp never makes it into the old farmhouse where you have arranged for it to be."

Since they didn't know Harmony was there, they thought it would be easy to destroy the lamp and therefore destroy Arty and Andora.

The two went back to the undertaker's office and took the lamp, placing it behind some bricks in the wall. They originally wanted to destroy the lamp, but this was not possible. They had placed the very protection upon the lamp which they now could not turn off. After replacing the bricks and sealing them, the two demons applauded themselves.

Harmony was not going to let them off that easy. She knew she couldn't do anything right now, but she would have to make sure the lamp was found. Moreover, she needed to trick Mordrid into believing that he could stop the inevitable from happening. He must be made to believe that he could, in fact, make slaves out of Andora and Arty.

The patch up job that Mordrid and Omar did was good enough to last centuries, but Harmony wanted the lamp found, just as it had in the natural course of history. She called upon help from the Heavens to slowly work at the concrete which held the stone in place so it would crumble and be noticed by the son of the undertaker. Then he would hold it up as a prop and tell the story his father loved to tell. History would not be changed.

Then Harmony got an idea. She knew that unlike she and all the Angels of Heaven, Mordrid, Omar and the other followers of Satan could only live each day. That meant they did not have the power of moving through time in the same manner as the Angels. They live for eternity or until the Master sees a reason to cast them into outer darkness, but they could not fine-tune. This meant Mordrid would not be able to know what the future would bring until the time came.

She also knew that Mordrid would not remember after a hundred and fifty years that Arty and Andora were the people he hoped to destroy. He knew them only as two of the many people he had tricked into slavery.

Harmony relied on this. If History was going to be changed by this, she would have known it. Mordrid was congratulating himself and moving on. No harm had been done.

Sure enough, the son of the undertaker found the lamp and the course of history went on as if Mordrid had never done a thing. The fact was that he only helped make sure the son did find that lamp, and Arty and Andora would find themselves in the old farmhouse where she found them. It haunted Harmony, though. The fact that Mordrid may become suspicious caused her to want to do more.

"Arty, I want you to do something," she stated flatly. Arty listened obediently as she laid out her plan. Then as part of her plan he sent Frank back to the ship to wait. When the time was right she had Henry and Arty—who was visible to all—talk about how Henry's future could be positive if he didn't do anything as foolish as to hold up the Tradesman County Bank.

After Henry had fallen asleep, Arty stood as if to go to the bathroom. He got a strange desperate look on his face, and then his face was a mask of terror. He faded out of sight and disappeared.

Omar was standing in the shadows watching. As Arty disappeared, he could hear his wail.

"It worked," he applauded. "We have destroyed the cowboy. Now the only thing Mordrid has to do is recreate someone to rob the bank and take the place of that rascal. He will have better luck with the replacement."

Harmony and Andora were watching as he hunted Mordrid and shared the news with him.

"They won't even know that it is still the same two people who will rob the bank," said Harmony. They will have no idea that you will still be Mordrid's downfall.

The ship had disappeared from the barn where it had been hidden, so the two demons were applauding themselves on their success. What they did not know was that the ship found itself with Frank and Arty inside right back where it had been before it headed away from the Earth.

"Frank, are you there?" asked the voice on the receiver.

"I'm here," answered Frank just as Arty had prompted. "We went through quite a meteor storm out here, but no damage was done."

"We lost contact for about five seconds," answered the voice from Earth. That kind of made us nervous."

"Not to worry," answered Frank. I'm still headed for Mars."

Mordrid would not know this because he could not look into the future. He could only live one day at a time.

While Arty and Frank headed toward the Mars Space Station, Harmony and Andora had to help Henry and they had to do it without his knowing it. This would prove to be a challenge.

However, it was a challenge that Harmony had faced many times. She simply did what she does best. She filled Henry's mind with love and compassion. He wondered where Arty and Frank had gone, but this was the old west. Cowboys would come and go unannounced all the time. He figured they just moved on.

With inspiration from Harmony, Henry began to see that something could be done to stop people like Haskins from abusing people. He could avenge his family's deaths by putting his energy into a crime-stopper's campaign.

"I'll find a place and run for town sheriff somewhere," he thought to himself. That same day he rode off toward the west to find a place where he might fulfill his dream. Andora and Harmony knew at this point that Dunham's life was no longer in danger.

Now they simply had to make sure that Mordrid would continue to congratulate himself for getting rid of Arty and Andora.

That would prove to be a challenge because Mordrid was taking no chances. He was watching for an opportunity to improve his position. He realized that unlike the Angels he could not move through time like people walk from one room to another. His future depended upon his changing it right now.

Mordrid realized that he would need to cause the person who saw Arty and Andora ride out of town in the wagon to become distracted. If they didn't see Andora in the wagon, the posse would not be riding up on the two and they would make a clean get-away. Then Mordrid would find someone else to recruit in their place and his condemnation would thereby be undone.

There was a cowboy who had just put his horse up for the night at the town livery stable. Mordrid distracted him by causing something to fall, just as he lit a match to smoke a cigar that caused a fire. Everyone came running to fight the blaze, including the man who would have seen Andora in the wagon the night

Arty robbed the bank. Because of the fire, the sheriff would not go to check out Dunham for several hours after the bank closed. This would mean Arty and Andora would live on. Mordrid congratulated himself on this accomplishment. If they lived on they would not be in the position that Omar had told him about.

Harmony knew of Mordrid's plans. She would not make it that easy for him. She had also been watching as Omar, per Mordrid's request, was busy working with a town prankster. It seems the wagon Arty would steal to get away in belonged to one David Morton. The prankster was a friend of his and knew he only used the wagon to ride home from work each evening, and that it would break down on the road home and curse him for the bad joke. Omar caused him to decide on some other way to play a joke on his friend. He decided to go to the friend's house and prop a bucket of water above his door so he would be soaked as soon as he pulled the door open.

Andora waited until Omar had finished his chore and then played the devil's advocate. She caused the prankster to think it would be so much more fun if the wagon broke down on the way home and then after a long exhausting walk David opened the door and was soaked. He went back to the wagon and sawed the bolt to insure it would break. Then he went home whistling to himself.

Since time was nothing more than a medium through which they could travel, the Angels saw the devastation of the fire. Harmony doubled back to the distraction of the cowboy in the livery stable. She inspired him to get a bucket of water to give to his horse before he lit that match. Sure enough Mordrid's distraction occurred and caused the cowboy to drop the lit match, but the bucket of water was there and he threw it upon the fire and the livery stable never went up in smoke.

All Mordrid knew was that he had failed. Harmony knew that she would have to make him think he had somehow changed history. Andora had an idea.

She went back to the time Arty told Frank about his past, but she caused a cosmic distraction so Arty's words became slurred. Omar thought he said his name was Arnold. Thus the two demons were not aware of who it was they were trying to stop.

Mordrid thought Arty and Andora were to take the place of Arnold and Ann. He had no idea that they were one and the same. Therefore, he proceeded with his plans to inspire the sidewinder that Arty had been to rob the bank. He felt that he had created so many possible changes in the future that one of them worked. He especially took pleasure in the fact that Arty had disappeared. This, he thought, was because Arty would never become an angel. He couldn't have known that Arty was on a ship with Frank floating through Space in the twenty second century.

Chapter 7 (Look Out Mars, Here Comes Arty!)

Frank found himself constantly looking back toward the Earth. He saw it looking smaller and smaller as he flew further into outer space, toward Mars. He faced the adventure with a feeling of hope that he had longed for all his life, but had given up on until the day Arty appeared before him.

He knew things that he could not share with the others of his time. He knew they would think him crazy and lock him away in an institution if he even tried. He lived in a world that had given up on a Creator. But the Master had not given up on them. There were still others like Frank that were ready to save.

Arty brought him out of his contemplation with a few facts about his mission.

"You need to fine-tune your course," he prompted. "It's about time to put this thing into overdrive. This should be a real thrill," Arty added. "You will now be going faster than any man has ever gone before."

Frank plotted his course with Arty's help and was soon headed directly toward The Space Station Mars.

Frank lay back in his reclining seat and grabbed some much needed sleep. It was at this point that a familiar voice startled Arty.

"You managed to do it," he chided. "I'll make you pay, you fool."

"Make me pay. Managed to do what?" Arty enquired. He found himself looking at Omar.

"You somehow sent Mordrid into Outer Darkness. I must make you pay for that."

"You can't," replied Arty. "I'm out of your reach. You know that a demon cannot overcome an angel of the Master. That's how Mordrid met his demise. I was there. It wasn't really me that sent Mordrid anywhere. It was in fact Harmony who beat him in the battle of concentration. He could not stand up against the powers of the Universe. The Master lets you exist because you serve a purpose. He can destroy you as easily."

"You're right," said Omar. "I can destroy Frank and his great mission, though. I will do that in the name of Mordrid."

"I will see you cast into Outer Darkness, in the name of the Master," countered Arty. "You had better think twice before you try anything." As he spoke he turned his attention to the Bible that lay by Frank's side. Omar grew nervous and backed away, but Arty knew he would need help. He only hoped his friends would wind up their chores in the past and join him soon.

Actually that Bible had become nothing more to the people of Frank's day than a fine piece of literature. It was regarded by many as a wonderful work of fiction. Most people had decided that there was no Creator. They were distracted by their scientific studies and had become surer, or at least they thought they were, that man and every living creature as well as the world itself was nothing more than a fluke of nature. They believed evolution was in itself, man's creator.

Arty had to prompt Frank to buy it and read it. With Arty's help, Frank would begin to learn that there was much more to life than man could see, feel, touch or taste.

Right now, it was the Bible that was holding Omar at bay, but Arty knew the demonic minds of these creatures. He wasn't sure how but he knew Omar would try to get around this obstacle. Arty wondered why he had suddenly lost contact with the Master. However, he knew he would be taken care of. The fact that Omar was still scared of the holy book was enough to let him know that he was under the Master's protection.

Omar was contemplating his next move. He soon came up with an idea and he knew just how he would accomplish it.

Omar reached out through the void of space and created a wormhole right in the path of Frank's ship.

"What's that?" Frank cried. That was the last anyone on Earth heard. The mission center went crazy. They had lost Frank for the second time and now they were getting nervous.

What Frank and Arty saw next was a meteor shower. It did not take long for Arty to realize that they had traveled into a completely different solar system and those meteors had the ability to crash the ship and put an end to Frank's work, not to mention his life.

It was then that Arty proved himself. He disappeared from Frank's side, but before Frank could panic, Arty's voice reassured him that he had things in control.

Arty pulled deep from the power of the Master every force he could and became a power shield for the space craft.

From inside, Frank kept flinching each time one of the floating pieces of space debris came close to the ship, but Arty simply willed it aside. The ship seemed to Frank to be making its own path through the meteor shower.

Omar was beside himself with anger. He had to destroy this human. He didn't know how, but he was consumed with hatred and hungry for revenge.

Frank watched as the shield disappeared from around the ship and Arty again became visible to him inside.

"Whew," exclaimed Arty. "That was hard work. Let me do some scouting around. We need to get you back to the solar system you started out in."

"Solar system I what?" Frank asked with perplexity. Arty had to explain what had just happened. Frank took it surprisingly well.

Another one of those meetings was about to occur. As Frank blinked an eye, Arty found himself standing alone with the Master. It was only now that Arty realized that though he had been here many times, he had never really seen the Master. He felt his presence, but he could not see him. Arty wondered why, so he asked.

"What do you look like?" he enquired. The Master's reply was that he had no form. He did not need one. He was in everything. When Arty looked perplexed the Master explained.

"I am the air that surrounds the Earth. I am the void in outer space. I am every wind that blows. I am storms, lightning, thunder, hurricanes, typhoons, tornados. I am the sunshine, the darkness, the waters of the sea. I am the very DNA that makes up every living creature, even man. I am you Arty. I am the first blossom in the spring and the last leaf to fall from the tree in the fall. I am spring, summer, fall and winter. A wise man once asked me long ago who I was and I answered, 'I am.' You cannot see me as a person, but you can see me in life anytime you look. Does that answer your question?"

Arty stood silently for a few moments. Then simply asked why the Master had summoned him.

"We need to decide where to go from here," replied the Master. "Omar would like to destroy Frank. You could easily get away from his quest for vengeance, but Frank will need your help. Let's see if we can fine-tune the past a little."

Suddenly, Arty found himself surrounded by what appeared to be TV screens. The Master advised him that they were, in fact, windows into any part of the past, present or future.

Arty found himself staring at one window. It was Mr. Dunham closing up the bank when a masked gunman wearing a mask came in waving his forty-five.

"That's me," Arty exclaimed. "That's me robbing that bank. Can we go back and change that?"

"You know that if we do we will also change the future," replied the Master.

Arty glanced over at another window and saw Andora and Harmony standing in the desert.

"What are they talking about?" Arty enquired.

"They're dealing with Mordrid and Omar," the Master answered. Arty watched for a minute then asked another question.

"Are they going to be able to take care of the problem?" the Master simply answered,

"You are still here, aren't you? That means they did what was required of them. If not, you or Frank or possibly both of you would no longer exist."

What Arty did not know, or at least was not paying attention, to was what Harmony was telling Andora.

"You know the best thing we have going for us is the fact that Mordrid, Omar and the other followers of the Prince of Darkness are rather stupid. It may seem that what we have done was a weak excuse for covering up Arty's blunder, but those creatures are easily led astray."

What she did not tell Andora was that she knew Mordrid was not overly bright, although he was paranoid enough that he would not take anything for granted. His greatest fear was the thought of being cast into Outer Darkness.

That fear was going to be the trump card in the twentieth century. It would lead to his demise. Mordrid would still hold the fear in the back of his mind that he had been out maneuvered by the Angels. This would cause him to do something dangerous like trying to desecrate the Holy Bible. This would not happen until he had captured the souls of Arty and Andora. It would be the very thing that would help them win the eternal forgiveness of the Master.

Now Harmony & Andora had to do multitasking. They had to be in constant touch with George and Allison to let them know that Frank was still safe. The two Angels also had another task which the Master had assigned them.

As they went about the duties assigned, Arty and Frank were working at getting back through the wormhole and finalizing the trip to Mars.

Omar was not going to help. He wanted revenge for the loss of his friend. As Frank and Arty worked at getting the ship back on it's rightful course, Frank saw a huge beast coming out of space. The black void of space seemed to disappear and it started to look like being in a plane flying over the earth in the early morning sun.

"What is that?" Frank asked in fear.

"Omar thinks he can intimidate us," responded Arty. "I'll show that sidewinder what intimidation is all about." Arty seemed to disappear from the seat next to Frank.

Frank's jaw dropped open at what he saw next. The monster was about twenty feet high. It looked like it was mostly head, arms and legs with no body to speak of. It had teeth that looked like they could bite through metal and it was snarling.

Then Frank swallowed hard, almost choking when he saw Arty. Arty was twenty feet tall, too.

"Wow!" was all Frank could utter. Arty was dressed like the old gun slinger he had been in the old west, but he was huge.

"Hey, Cubby," he yelled. Frank didn't know how he was talking in space, but he was. The monster turned toward Arty to attack.

Arty drew his sidearm and fired, making a loud bang. The monster disappeared and the space around Frank became black and void again.

Arty reappeared in the seat next to Frank. When Frank asked why the change in color, Arty explained that the monster was surrounded with its own air pocket much as the earth was surrounded by the air.

"I showed him," Arty praised himself. "Big bang and all."

Omar was so shocked by Arty's big display of heroics that he pulled back. He wasn't going to go the way of Mordrid if he could help it.

"I don't think that demon will bother us for a while," Arty said. "Let's find that wormhole and get you back on the way to Mars.

It didn't take long before they had guided the ship back on its path and passed back into the solar system from which they came.

There was a cheer at the space center on Earth when they again regained contact with Frank's ship. There was also baffled look on the face of one of the people who was in charge of plotting the course and tracking the navigation of Frank's ship.

"Sir," announced Ray Hucklebee. The commander turned and responded. He could not help but notice the confused look on Hucklebee's face.

"Sir, in the twelve hours that we lost contact with the space craft, it seems to have traveled about three quarters of the way to Mars."

There was a time of recalculating and reevaluating of the figures. Nobody could understand how, but Frank had somehow traveled a long way in a short period of time. Frank explained the fact that there were wormholes in space.

"I don't know how, but I slipped into one and when I came out I was here," he said.

Arty was relaxing. They were coming up on Mars and He and Frank were enjoying the close-up view of the red planet.

Meanwhile, George's ship was taking off from Earth to follow Frank.

Chapter 8 (Women Angels Are Great At Multi-tasking)

Meanwhile, in the old west, Harmony and Andora had wrapped all but the constant monitoring of Mordrid and Omar.

It was then that the Master called them for a meeting. While monitoring the two demons, they had another job to do in the twentieth century.

"A man will commit a murder," the Master told them. "I would not involve myself in this except for the fact that he must be caught. He will be sentenced to death. Your job is to save his never dying soul. You will also save the souls of some other men who will die in prisons on the planet Earth. They were good men who made bad mistakes. The laws of the governing powers of the country will sentence them to life in prison; some will even be sentenced to death. The man you must help is a detective. He will put this man in prison and though it will cost him his earthly life, it will save his spirit for eternity. Oh yes," the Master explained. "You must work without his knowing you are there. This man leans toward atheistic, so he must not know you are guiding him until he begins to question his own non-belief."

With that he sent the angels on their way. The hardest part for them to take was standing by and watching the murder take place, knowing they were forbidden to change it.

It was a beautiful spring day when a beautiful strawberry blonde and a man in a business suit walked out of a hotel on the west side of New York City.

"When are you going to tell Joe that you're in love with me?" asked Lynne.

Sarah let out a sigh. She wasn't looking forward to this. She couldn't help the fact that her love for Joe had all but died. She did love him, but she couldn't think of spending the rest of her life with him. Joe was to demanding. Everything had to be his way and she could live her whole life as if everything that she was had to conform to his way of thinking.

"I will tell him today," she promised. "I'll tell him this evening." She kissed Lynne, who flagged down a cab.

"Call me when you get a chance," he said as he got into the cab. She turned and walked toward a delicatessen to get a cup of coffee.

It was about fifteen minutes past nine in the morning when Detective Jack McCausty was called to the crime scene.

With lights flashing, he pulled up behind another police which was already on the scene.

"What do we have?" he asked. The officer took him around the corner into the alley. They had not removed the body from the garbage dump, yet. They were waiting for him.

"Have you dusted for fingerprints?" Jack asked. The officer affirmed that they had done so and there were more fingerprints at one place or another all over the place.

"I don't know if that will help you, though," he added. "We haven't found anything in the data base yet. God alone knows how many people come up and down this alley. You're gonna have fun trying to check every one of these. That is, of course, if we do find any of them in our data base.

"Who found the body?" enquired Jack.

"Those two over there," answered the officer pointing to two young boys standing wide-eyed by the corner. Jack walked over toward them.

"What you fella's doing here?" he asked. The smaller boy shrank away from the detective. The other one explained that they were just looking for treasure.

"Treasure in a dumpster?" Jack asked in disbelief. "You must be hard up for treasure. Tell me this," he asked. "Did you see anyone coming into this alley?"

"No sir," the boy answered. "Honest, sir, we would never hurt that lady. We just found her," He said more loudly now. He was really stressed out and Jack could tell.

"Hold on, Son," he soothed. "Nobody thinks you did anything wrong. What time did you find her here?"

"I don't know," the boy answered. "I don't have a watch. It was about a half hour ago, though."

Jack thanked the boys and went back to the officers and medical people who were now pulling the body out of the dumpster.

"Do you think she was on drugs?" he asked.

"We won't know until the M.E. does an exam," answered the officer. "It doesn't look like it, though. There are no bruise marks or needle punctures on the body. Of course we have not had a chance to really examine it."

Jack's next stop was the delicatessen. Nobody there could tell him anything. He then went up and down the street, asking if anyone had seen anything. He even went into a bar across the street. The officers had taken a picture of the girl after dragging her out of the dumpster. Jack showed the picture, asking everyone if they had seen anything. Everyone said they had not noticed anything out of the ordinary.

There was something in the back of his mind that kept nagging at Jack, although he didn't know why.

He found a picture of Joe Morton in the girl's wallet. He also found her driver's license. Jack went to the address on the license.

There was no answer when he knocked so Jack knocked louder. A neighbor came to the door and looked down the hall to where Jack was standing.

"There won't be anybody there until this evening," the neighbor offered. "They are both at work."

"One of them may be," Jack answered. He walked over to the neighbor. "This girl was murdered this morning. Do you know where her husband works?"

"You mean her boyfriend?" corrected the neighbor. "These kids these days don't bother with getting married anymore."

"I get your point," Jack said. "Do you know where her boyfriend works?"

"Down on 51st. street. He works in a pizza joint down there. I can't remember the name. He works at a place called Papa Jowls or something like that."

"What's His name?" asked the detective.

The next stop for Jack was 51st. Street. Papa Jowls was a family-owned pizza parlor. The owner was a round sort of fella. Somehow, that did not surprise Jack. The man looked like he might have eaten as many pizzas as he sold.

"What can I do for you?" he enquired of Jack.

"I'm Detective Jack McCausty," he said by way of introduction while showing his badge. "Do you have a Joe Morton working for you?"

The man was a little taken by surprise. He swallowed hard and requested what the detective wanted with the man. Jack simply asked the question again.

"Yes," answered the parlor owner after about a half minute. "He's not in some kind of trouble is he?"

"We need to talk to him," Jack stated flatly. The man turned over his shoulder and shouted for Joe to come to the front.

"Coming," Joe answered and he came out to the front. Jack held his badge. He couldn't be sure, but he swore he could see fear in the man's eyes; when the police come looking for anybody, they get a little apprehensive.

"What is it?" asked Joe. Jack's answer was that the man might want to sit down. Then he explained the fact that they found Sarah's body downtown.

"We will need you to identify her body for us," he explained. Also, we need to know if she had any family here."

"Her folks live in Chicago," Joe answered and he gave Jack their phone number. Jack had been in homicide for quite a few years. One thing he never relished was the chore of telling a mother and father that they had lost a child. Somehow, it wasn't easy whether the child was six or thirty-six.

"Where were you this morning between eight and nine?" he asked Joe.

"Stuck in traffic, on my way to work," Joe answered.

Jack asked all the usual questions. What route did he take? How bad was the traffic? Did anyone see him?

Somehow something told Jack that this man was hiding something. The problem was that he could not prove anything. Stuck in traffic in New York City was not hard to prove. Jack himself hated the early morning rush-hour traffic.

"When did you see Sarah last?" he asked. Joe's answer was that she didn't come home the night before. When asked why he had not reported her missing, Joe answered that she often would stay at a friend's house. He thought she simply forgot to call.

"Why wouldn't she call and tell you she was staying over?" asked Jack.

"She might have been drinking," Joe replied. Jack asked for this friend's name. Joe tried to duck the question by stating that she had several girlfriends that she often partied with.

"Listen," he finally sighed. "We have an open relationship. We both agreed that we would give each other free time. When she doesn't come home I take it for granted she's partying with someone."

"Names!" Jack spoke in a way that demanded an answer. So he walked away with about eight girls' names and addresses. Joe pointed them out, though that he had no idea which if any of these girls had seen her the night before.

"This guy is making it up as he goes," Jack muttered to himself as he walked back to his car.

Now he had eight visits to make, but first he had to stop by the M.E.'s office and see what, if anything he may have found.

What he found out at the Medical Examiner's office was pretty much what he had suspected. No signs of drug abuse. The only signs of violence were the bruises around her neck. She had been strangled and the person strangling her was wearing gloves made of imitation leather.

That's when Jack got a call from his chief. When he walked into the office he already knew it was to replace his long-time partner, who had just retired, but he had a surprise that he was not ready for.

Standing to the right of the chief was a beautiful woman. She had dark brown hair and blue eyes and she was dressed in a business suit.

"This is your new partner," the chief said by way of introduction. "Her name is Audrey Shoemaker.

Jack was going to say something when the chief gave him one of his 'don't go there' looks and Jack decided he would have to make the best of it. He didn't like the thought of working with a female cop.

He spent several hours bringing Audrey up to date on the case they were working, and then they went off to finish the call list Jack had made.

Audrey did not say anything in the car. She seemed to know that Jack was fighting with the problem of having a female by his side. She couldn't figure if it were that he was a macho sort of guy or if he was simply worried that she may get hurt. She figured anything she said right now would not be much help. She could only hope that he would learn to trust her as a fellow cop.

When they got to the home of Sandra Madigan, Frank was given food for thought.

He was getting nowhere with this lady. His surly attitude was simply a turn-off to her. She decided to simply swap put-downs with him instead of answering his questions.

Audrey took a deep breath. She figured this male chauvinistic jerk-off would call him to task, but she knew there were things to be learned.

"Jack, would you mind if we ladies talked alone for a few minutes?" she asked. Jack wanted say no, but he was taken aback by her request.

"I'll be in the car," he muttered as he walked out the door. Audrey looked over to the other woman.

"Can I call you Sandy?" she requested.

"Actually, that's what my friends call me," answered Sandy. "Look, I really don't know what happened to Sarah and I don't appreciate some wise guy coming around treating me like I'm a piece of meat."

"He can be a jerk," Audrey agreed. "He's just trying to find out some background on Sarah. We've been told you know her well. Nobody is trying to say you were in any way a part of this, but if there is any background you can tell me, it may help find out what happened."

"What kind of background? You mean like her sex life? I don't understand what you want to find out from me," Sandy responded.

"How were things between Sarah and Joe Morton?" asked the detective. Sandy looked into her folded hands.

"O.K., I guess," she said. Then she studied her hand some more. When she looked up into Audrey's eyes, Audrey could not help but notice Sandy's eyes were misty.

"Look," she said. "I don't want to create any problems for Joe; things between them would have been fine if he hadn't been so possessive. If she stopped at the coffee shop for a cup with me after work, he grilled her as to why she didn't come home sooner. It was like he was completely sure she was always out with somebody else."

"Was she?" asked Audrey. It made since that if this man was so super possessive he may have drove her to someone else.

"I guess I shouldn't tell you, but she was seeing a guy on the sly. That was only because Joe was becoming such a pain in the ass."

"Do you know his name?" Audrey enquired. All Sandy could tell her was his first name was Lynn.

"If you think of anything else, give me a call," requested Audrey, handing Sandy her card. Then she said goodbye and walked out to the car.

Fortunately for both of them, Jack had a chance to cool off by the time she got there. Moreover, he knew he wasn't getting anywhere with the lady. His old partner used to do much the same thing as Audrey. On occasion he did the same, himself.

"What did you find out?" he asked, purposely not looking her way. Audrey turned to look at him though, and explained everything that went on with the two ladies after he left. She did leave out the part about calling Jack an Ass.

In spite of himself, Jack was impressed. Maybe there were times when having a woman for a partner might come in handy. Still, though Jack was concerned about how she would handle a life or death situation.

"I have a feeling this guy is the Perp," he said. "I can't explain why, but call it a hunch.

"Are we going to check out the other people now?" asked Audrey. Jack stared out the window as he drove.

"Yes. I think maybe you would be better equipped to handle the questioning. I guess I just don't think like a woman."

Audrey smiled to herself. Jack took her back to the precinct and dropped her off at her own car.

"I'm going back to the hotel," he said. "Maybe they can shed some light on this lover boy of the vic."

Audrey went to visit the other girls on the list and Jack headed for the hotel. He got out of his car and went inside. Jack didn't notice the man standing across the street watching as he headed for the lobby. The man, Peter Brady, knew him as the detective because he had seen him asking questions after the murder of that girl. Peter had seen what happened, but he choose not to get involved, so he went into the bar and had a few beers without letting anybody know he had seen anything

Now he was feeling something completely out of character for him. He was feeling guilty. He did not like cops. Peter had a wrap sheet for pushing dope on the streets. Why was he feeling so bad about staying out of this mess? He couldn't understand what was nagging at him but it was.

Meanwhile, Jack went up to the desk and showed the girl's picture to the clerk

"Oh, yeah, that's the girl that got killed out front," exclaimed the clerk.

"Did she ever come in here?" asked Jack. The clerk seemed a little hesitant to speak, but finally swallowed and answered.

"Yes," he said. "She's been in quite a few times over the last few months with some guy. I got the feeling she was seeing him on the sly. They would rent a room, stay for three or four hours and then leave. I didn't want to poke my nose into other people's business so I never asked questions.

"Who paid?" asked Jack.

"She did, with her credit card," the desk clerk answered. "The guy usually stayed out in the lobby. I don't know who they thought they were fooling; they acted like just two people who happened to be here at the same time. It didn't take a rocket scientist to tell they were together.

"Did you ever get his name?" asked Jack

"No," answered the clerk. "Like I said, they were acting very sly but not sly enough."

"Would you recognize this guy if you saw him again?" Jack asked next.

The clerk said yes and Jack asked him to come down to the precinct to talk to the sketch artist.

Chapter 9 (Andorra's Task)

Time is just a dimension to the Master and fine-tuning the events of history kept things going for people like Jack, Frank and everyone else on the Earth and beyond.

It was now Andorra's turn to do a job on her own. She was called to the Master who was standing at the heavenly windows watching Jack and Audrey through one window, Frank and George through another. Andorra looked through that window and noticed that by now George was almost ready to dock with Frank's ship which would add part two to the space station.

"Harmony will keep a watch on the Detective for the time being," said the Master. "I want you to take a look through this window."

He directed Andorra toward one of many windows which reflected different times in the past, present and the future. All were the same to the Master.

"This goes back to the time you and Arty were inside that lamp sleeping. There was a woman who living in the time of the Second World War who is contemplating suicide. She must not. It is from her seed that Frank will eventually be born. You must help her. She needs to know someone cares."

He went on to explain that Andorra would have to appear in the form of a living person for this.

"Here's how it works," he began. "You pretend that you are in a horrible depression. She is a good woman. She will try to help you. By doing so, it will give her life new meaning and help her over this time of depression."

"How will I do that?" asked Andorra. The Master simply told her to use her wits.

"You are a good person, too," he explained. "Let her see that her life can make a difference and she will know there is a reason to live."

With that he sent Andorra on her way, but not before he reminded her to pay a visit to Allison. He explained that George was almost to the point of docking with Frank and Allison would be taking off from Earth.

"She will need your support," the Master advised.

Andorra contemplated for a second and then finally asked the question that she had wanted to ask from the moment she became an Angel.

"Master, how is it that we can be doing so many things, past, present and future at the same time. I remember when I was the girl friend of a bank robber when things seemed to go on forever. I still remember those long waits when Arty was robbing a bank. Time seemed to stand still. Now I have traveling through time like I was getting on a shuttle."

"Think on it!" advised the Master. When you were flesh and blood you were contained by a physical body which demanded that time have a sequence. Now you are not flesh and blood. Now, you are a spirit. Your realm is my realm. We see time as another dimension."

Andorra did not ask for more. She went to minister to Allison as she readied for take-off in the Twenty-Second Century.

Upon seeing Allison safely rocketing toward the space station Mars, Andorra went to her next assignment.

Standing on a pier, looking into the water was a woman. She was twenty-two years old. She was a pretty woman, but there was an awful sadness in her eyes. She was staring down at the cold water of the ocean.

Andorra knew what she was doing. Rita Malone was trying to work up the courage to jump and end her life. Furthermore, Andorra knew why. The man she loved had left her. Rita wanted to marry and have children. He wanted nothing to do with it. He found himself another woman to hold—a woman who would not pressure him for marriage or children. In short, he wanted someone to lie with at night. He wanted someone to make love to, but he did not want the responsibility of being more than a stud.

This left Rita feeling used and abused. It had stripped her of her dignity, since she had slept with the man many times, thinking he would always love her.

As she stood staring into the water Andora faded into sight just to her side.

Rita had not seen her coming so she was surprised that someone was standing to her side as she contemplated the jump into the dark, cold water below.

"Why do you want to jump?" Andorra asked

"You wouldn't understand," was the answer Rita was willing to give. Andorra took it upon herself to fill in the blanks.

"You know this guy is not the only guy in the world and he is a bit of a pig," Andorra said bluntly.

"If he only knew what he was walking away from, he would wish he were a better man," she added.

Rita turned to her. She didn't know this woman and she couldn't figure how this woman knew much about her.

"How do you know about Ray?" she asked. Andorra didn't tell. She simply went on with what she was saying.

"If you jump off this pier," she said. "You will be throwing a very promising life away. There was a sudden intake of breath as Rita realized that this woman knew what she was contemplating.

"You don't want to go through with this," Andorra prompted; even as she spoke she knew what was coming next.

Rita looked at her for a few seconds and then returned her gaze to the water. Then everything seemed to go black.

The next thing she knew she was plummeting into the waters of the ocean below.

From the fall off the pier the water felt like hitting concrete and even before she went under she truly passed out.

Rita was surprised when she woke up. She was lying on the beach. Rita sat up and looked around. There stood Andorra.

"Now, what do you think you accomplished by that?" asked Andorra. "Did you think this would somehow hurt anyone besides yourself?"

"You mean Ray?" asked Rita. It was a ret oracle question. "Yes, I had hoped he would find it in his heart to be sorry for my death. I guess I can't do anything right." Then she stared at Andorra's eyes

"How did you get down here?" she asked. "You were on the pier. Did you drag me out of the water? Why didn't you let me end this useless life?"

"Sweetheart," Andorra began, sound a bit like someone's mother. "Try to pinch yourself.

Rita brought a hand up to pinch her arm. Her eyes were wide with fear when she realized she couldn't even touch herself. This made Andorra think back to the day in the undertaker's office when Arty found he couldn't draw his gun.

"Am I dead?" asked Rita.

"Isn't that what you wanted?" Andorra asked in return. Rita stared at Andorra and then turned her gaze to the ocean for a spell.

"Well," prompted Andorra. "That was what you wanted, right?"

"Yes," answered Rita. "That is what I wanted; if I'm dead why am I still here? Is this purgatory? What's happening to me?"

"You are about to see all the things you might have experienced if you had only been brave enough to not jump off that pier," Andora advised.

"Let's take a stroll through time." Andorra raised her hand and Rita saw the beach fade into history and in its place was a shopping mall. There was a man walking along. He was a good looking man. Rita was certain he could have any woman he wanted. He was much more handsome than Ray.

"This guy would make quite a catch, wouldn't he?" Andorra asked. "He'll never marry, though. He will live a long life, but his soul mate will never show up.

Before Rita could ask what she meant by that Andorra went on with her dissertation.

"Let me show you what could have been," she said. Once again she raised her hand and although they were still standing in the same Mall, Rita noticed a woman walking beside him. To her amazement, the woman was Rita. In her arms was a baby boy and he had a toddler on his shoulders.

Then Rita and the children faded away and the man was walking alone, looking lonely.

"You know, sometimes we forget how much our lives can affect others," Andorra said. "We also don't know how many blessings we can deprive ourselves of. Didn't you always want a man who loved you and children?" she asked. It really wasn't so much a question as it was a reflection.

"Yes," Rita answered. Why couldn't I meet this man instead of Ray?"

"You could have, if you would have given yourself a chance. Ray wasn't the only man in the world. Love hurts sometimes, but faith can heal those hurts. The secret is keeping the faith," Andorra continued. "You wanted to jump off that pier. By doing so, you deprived yourself the very thing you wanted most and you deprived this man of a happiness that he will never know without you. Of course, you also deprived two children of the right to live. I'll tell you a little secret. From the love of you and Robert would come someone who would change the world in a very positive way. I guess the world will have to just muddle through without that change.

"I guess I was too quick to want to end the pain," Rita lamented. "I guess I should have trusted God a little more. I guess I thought the pain of having Ray leave me was the greatest pain I would ever know. I was wrong. I'm living that pain now. I guess you call this living, but then, I'm dead."

"It gets worse," advised Andorra. When she again raised her hand, they were standing at the same pier where they started. They were watching Robert as he stared into the cold dark water below. Andorra didn't have to tell Rita what he was thinking. Rita knew the look. She had the same look in her eyes before she jumped.

"Oh, don't let him do this," she implored. "He has much to live for. Please don't let him jump."

"He won't," Andorra reassured her. "But, he will contemplate it over and over again. His life will be empty and he will feel useless."

As she spoke Robert turned slowly and walked away, leaving Rita and Andorra alone on the pier.

"God forgive me," she cried as tears welled up in her eyes. "I have committed a horrible sin. I never knew my life would mean anything to so many people."

"What sin?" asked Andorra.

"I jumped from that pier," answered Rita. I had no right to give up so easily. I deserve whatever punishment God has in store for me, but please help Robert." Andorra raised her hand one more time and Rita saw black.

When she came too, she was not surprised to find herself on the pier. She looked for Andorra but she didn't see her. She did hear her voice, telling her to pinch herself.

"Ouch," she exclaimed. Then she looked up at the heavens. She was still alive. Once more, she heard Andorra's voice.

"Go and live your life. You will meet someone who will love you more than himself. You will have children and you will make a positive difference in the lives of people who you will never know. One man walked away from you. That's his loss. Another will become your soul mate for life.

"I'm still alive," Rita practically shouted. I can still find love. Oh, thank you Lord. Thank you my God."

With that, Andorra went back to check on how Harmony and the detectives were doing.

Chapter 10 (The Case)

When Andorra joined Harmony she was applauded by the mother Angel.

"You saw?" asked Andorra. Then, she reminded herself that they could all be in different places at the same time. They could even be in different times at the same time.

Andorra was not overly surprised by the fact that things had not changed since she left Harmony. Jack was with the hotel clerk and the sketch artist, getting a picture of the man who was seen with Sarah before her murder.

While he went back to the hotel to ask anyone who may know the identity of the man, Audrey was busy questioning the other women on the list about who Sarah may have been seeing. She got pretty much the same story from each person she talked to until she asked Joyce McCauley, a close friend of Sarah's.

"She asked me not to tell anyone this," Joyce began. "But, she's dead now. I don't think I am violating her trust now. I must say that I don't believe Lynn would hurt her.

"Lynn who?" questioned Audrey.

"Lynn Morgan. They loved each other, but Audrey was afraid to tell her boyfriend, Joe, that she wanted to break off their relationship."

"Why was she afraid?" Audrey prompted. Joyce told her that Joe Morton had an awful temper and had threatened her in a manner of speaking if she ever left him.

"What did he say in the way of a threat?" asked the detective. Joyce didn't know. She said Sarah had told her several times that the man she thought she loved turned out to be a manipulative man who wanted everything his way and would not consider her feelings.

When Audrey headed back to the precinct she contemplated what the witness had told her. Now, it seemed she had two possible suspects.

Audrey shared what she had learned with Jack. The two of them didn't have to look far to find Joe. They already had his address.

"I had nothing to do with her murder," exclaimed Joe. "I loved her. Why are you trying to pin this on me.

"Where were you on that morning between eight and nine?" Joe asked once again.

"Look, you asked me already and I told you. I was stuck in traffic. Please stop wasting your time and find the person who hurt her. I hear she was seeing someone at that hotel. Maybe, he was the one who did it."

The two detectives shared a look. So, Joe knew about Sarah's affair. They didn't say anything. They didn't have enough to get a warrant so they thanked Joe for his time and went back to the car.

"So, he knew," said Jack and Audrey almost in the same breath. Jack looked at her and smiled

"Goes to motive," said Audrey

"And," began Jack, "The man has no alibi, but we still don't have enough to pin a murder charge on him."

"Maybe we should check out this Lynn Morgan," suggested Audrey. There were about eighteen listings of Lynn Morgan in the New York phone book, so the two decided to go back to Joyce with the sketch to see if it was in fact the man Sarah was seen with at that hotel.

They found it was. They also found after some talk that Joyce knew more about the man than she had originally told Audrey. She knew where he worked.

The two went to a small advertising firm on the west side and asked for him.

When Lynn came to them he looked like he hadn't slept for several nights. He looked tired and dejected.

"You asked for me?' he enquired. Upon asking some more questions the two detectives got him to open up.

"Look," he began. "We were seeing each other but I didn't kill her. I loved her. I wanted her to dump that fool she was with and I would have given her a life with me."

"Maybe, you loved her so much that you couldn't stand the idea of her going home to this fool," offered Audrey. "Maybe, you gave her a choice and she didn't love you as much as you did her. Maybe, you figured if you couldn't have her to yourself you make sure no man did. I've seen it all before."

"Audrey," Jack interrupted. "Let's not fool around with so many maybes. The poor man loved this woman.

"I'm going to get a cup of coffee," said Audrey as she stood. "Would you like some?" she asked the suspect. Lynn declined but Jack said he would like one. Audrey gave him a steamy look as she walked to the door.

"Next thing, you'll want me to do your laundry," she huffed as she went out of the room."

Jack smiled to himself. The two were playing good cop, bad cop in hopes of getting a confession out of this guy. However, something kept nagging at Jack. He didn't truly believe this was the man. His money was on Joe.

"Look," he began. "If this was an accident or something that happened before you could contain yourself, we can get the D.A. to come down on the charges. After all, a man will do some strange things out of love."

"I would have killed myself before I would have hurt Sarah. Look man, I'm going to have to live the rest of my life without the woman I love. Why would I even want to hurt her, knowing that I would never kiss her lips again? Even if she was afraid of that rat she was with," Lynn continued, "Just being with her when I could hold her in my arms for a few hours, was better than never making love to her again."

The door opened and Audrey walked in with two cups of coffee. She set one in front of Jack and took a sip from hers.

She had dropped the good cop, bad cop deal. She really believed what she had heard through the sound system from the other room.

They sent Lynn on his way and headed back to their desks to contemplate what they could from the situation.

"My money is on this Morgan, fellow," said Audrey. Jack stared at the notes of what they had already found out and simply nodded. Then he looked straight into Audrey's eyes for the first time since they met.

"You know something?" he asked. Audrey didn't respond. She was struck by the fact that he was looking into her eyes. Joe simply continued.

"You and I will make a great team," he said with a smile. Audrey wasn't sure how to handle this. For the first time since she met him, she found herself feeling defensive. The strange thing about it was the fact that this was the first sign of friendship from Jack. That was something she was not prepared for. It made her nervous. Then she realized that the reason for that nervousness was the excitement. She, for the first time had to admit that she was attracted to this man.

What was equally strange was that he was also attracted to her and now for the first time he was admitting it to himself and to her.

The two Angels stood in the background giving each other the High Five. They wanted these two to find one another, even if it were not part of the reason for their visit to this time in history.

"You don't think the Master will be upset with us, do you?" Andorra asked. Harmony dismissed it with a wave of her hand.

"He doesn't always say everything he wants done. They just seem to happen," she said. "He calls it fine-tuning."

"Fine-tuning," Andorra repeated almost in the form of a question. Harmony smiled and they stood in the shadows.

"You got any plans for dinner, tonight?" Jack asked.

"I was just going back to my apartment and grab something there," Audrey answered.

"How 'bout having dinner with me tonight?" asked Jack. "I know a real nice little Italian restaurant."

Her answer was a yes and their date was set. The Angels left them to do some more fine-tuning. They had been working on the mind of the man who was walking into the bar across the street when Sarah was attacked.

His name was Arnold Moats. He had a rap sheet and he did not like the police. It was for that reason that he had not come forward to tell what he saw that night. Although he didn't see the murder, his information would have cleared Lynn. He preferred not to get involved. Now, however, he was finding himself thinking that he really should. This really bothered him. He had never cared much about anyone but himself.

"Good Lord," he thought to himself. "I'm developing a conscience." No matter how he tried he could not shake the feeling that he needed to call someone's attention to what he saw that night.

After work, Jack and Audrey each went home and took showers. They had agreed that Jack would come by to pick Audrey up at seven.

Audrey found herself not only showering, but looking for something super attractive to wear. She even took the time to splash on some perfume before Jack got there. She was humming to herself. When she realized that she was going to all this trouble, she found herself chuckling. She had not bothered with such feminine stuff for many years.

When the doorbell rang she ran for the door like it was prom night. She was almost breathless when she saw Jack standing there wearing a suit and tie.

Jack was equally surprised to see Audrey looking more beautiful than he already thought she was.

"You're beautiful," he told her.

"I bet you say that to all the girls," she countered, while the look in her eyes told him she was thrilled to hear it.

"Nope," he retorted. "I can't remember the last time I said that."

For a while the two talked about the case they were working. They even shared some stories with each other about other cases they had worked. One might get the idea they were just a couple of guys eating together.

Then Jack changed the subject. As they were eating he suddenly took her by surprise by asking a question which she was not sure she wanted to answer.

"How come a beautiful lady like you isn't married?" he asked. Audrey deliberated for a spell.

"I almost did, once," she said. "It didn't work out. How come you're still single?"

"You first," said Jack. Audrey explained that the man she thought she would love forever turned out to be a control freak.

"He wanted me to quit my job and be a stay at home wife," she explained. "When I told him I wanted to keep working, he said he couldn't live with me that way. So, I told him we were better apart. Now, about you!"

She said that kind of in the form of a demand. Jack took a bite of spaghetti and sighed.

"My old man was a bit of a rat," he explained. "My mom finally divorced him and we lived alone. To tell you the truth, I don't know how she stayed with him as long as she did. I never wanted to be in the position to hurt anyone like he hurt her, and I never wanted to be hurt. I guess that's why I built a wall around my feelings. You seemed to break through that wall, Audrey. I didn't want to fall in love with you, but I couldn't stop it. To tell you the truth, I'm kind of scared. I hope we can build a life together."

"Are you proposing?" asked Audrey. Jack blushed. He hadn't realized how it sounded until she asked that question. There was a long pregnant pause. Jack finally broke the silence with a soft answer.

"Yeah, that is what I have wanted to ask you from the first time I laid eyes on you in the chiefs' office."

Audrey quietly put her fork down on the table. Suddenly she didn't feel hungry. She looked into his eyes. Tears were fighting to erupt from her eyes.

"This is so sudden," she answered quietly. "I wasn't ready for this so soon.

"So soon?" Jack prompted, his eyes pleading with hers.

"I think I have loved you from the beginning too, but I thought things would go a little slower. Man, Jack I'm kinda dizzy."

"You don't need to answer now. I've waited this long for you and I can wait longer," he offered

Suddenly Audrey didn't want to wait and now tears were flowing freely from her eyes.

"I hope those are happy tears," Jack crooned. Audrey assured him in between sniffles that they were definitely happy tears.

After dinner Jack took Audrey home. At her door he took her hands in his.

"I'll see you in the morning," he said. Audrey looked deeply into his eyes. She wanted him to kiss her. Suddenly he took her into his arms and they shared a long passionate kiss. It took all his will power to end it.

"Bye," he said softly. Audrey leaned forward and kissed him again. Somehow he managed to reign in his desire. Audrey went inside and as soon as the door was shut she fell back against it.

"Don't forget to lock your door," Jack said through the door. He heard the lock turn and went outside to find his car.

Chapter 11 (A Heavy Work Load)

Jack drove home and went to bed. Audrey also went to bed. They both would dream of each other. Neither of them cared about the work load they would have the next day.

Andorra and Harmony had no rest, but then Angels don't need rest. They also had a heavy work load.

They were called to the Master and told to concentrate on the happenings in the twenty-second century.

Frank and George had successfully docked and prepared their portion of the space station and were now waiting as Allison headed near to docking her portion of this great space station.

There were three more ships that had been sent from Earth to dock and complete the space station. No man knew just why this space station was so important, but they would know.

Andorra and Harmony rejoined Arty and were made aware that another Angel, their old friend, Gabriel, would be there with them as part of the next section which was piloted by Stewart Graham.

Stewart was another person who had been searching for something to believe in. Gabriel had come to him just after Frank took off into Space with his section of the Space station.

Stew had just lost his wife to cancer. They had been married a little over a year and she was never with child. His dreams seemed to be smashed when she died. The thing that haunted him most was that he knew no words to ease her pain and he blamed himself for his inability to save her.

Stew had lain awake many nights dreaming of the times when he held her in his arms, only to awaken and feel the horror of knowing that he would never again touch, caress or know her. He wanted her so much that he would have given his own life to bring her back.

Before he met Gabriel, he had no hope of anything. He was one of many who had given up on the Master. Jesus Christ, to him, was no more than a swear word.

One night as he slept, he dreamed that Mary Jane came to him. They held each other, caressed one another. Their kisses were long and passionate. That was when he woke up, alone.

Stew sat up. He looked around, hoping to see her again. He was ready to commit suicide when Gabriel made himself visible. Stew was scared.

"Are you an Alien?" he stammered. Gabriel smiled and slowly walked toward him.

"Some have said I was," he answered. "In a manner of speaking, they are probably right—I am not the kind of Alien you think. I am an Angel of the living God.

"I don't believe in those superstitions," Stew retorted. Gabriel smiled.

"Explain what I am and why I am here," he said as walked one more step closer to Stew.

"You're a dream. I was just dreaming of Mary, but my wonderful dream has become a nightmare.

"What if I told you that you will see Mary again?" asked Gabriel. He couldn't help but notice tears welling in Stews eyes. "What if I told you that she is with the Master and you can be, too?" he went on.

"What if I told you that you would first become a part of the salvation of the elect? Those people who are still alive on Earth who believe in God. You could be one of the people who trust in him even in this time of mistrust.

"I could see Mary Jane again?" Stew asked as if he had not heard another word Gabriel had said.

"You can," he answered. "She is waiting for you."

That was the beginning—just as Arty had done with Frank, Andorra had done with Allison and Harmony had done with George.

After all the training and what seemed to take forever, Stew was a part of the team headed for the new Space Station.

Meanwhile Allison was in radio contact with Frank and George. They prompted her as she maneuvered her ship toward the docking bay.

There was a slight tremor as her portion of the space station came in contact. Then they all went about the task of sealing the joint and pressurizing the hallway leading from her portion to theirs.

Finally everything checked out and they opened the doors, being careful to slowly equalize the pressure in all portions of the ship.

When this was done, George radioed back to Earth that everything was go and Allison came running through the doors into Frank's waiting arms. Actually, she wasn't running. She was sort of floating into his arms.

"How many times have we said I could float into your arms on earth, meaning we are so much in love," asked Frank. "This time we really are floating. I love you. It's good to hold you again," he crooned.

"Yeah," was all Allison had to say.

It was about two months later when Stew and his craft radioed that he was ready to dock.

The docking went without a hitch and they soon had equalized the cabins and opened the door and one more portion of the space ship was on board.

Then there came another and another until the final piece was added and the space station was completed.

As those on board the space station celebrated, the angels were called to the Master for a debriefing.

"You must ready these people for the unexpected," he advised. "They will need to know that what will seem to the people on Earth to be a catastrophe is truly a blessing for all."

He refused to tell more than that. He reminded Harmony and Andorra that they had unfinished business in the twentieth century.

Then he called Gabriel in for a private meeting. They had much to discuss.

"As I have told you from the very beginning, my son & I have had special plans for the selected ones from all of history. This goes back to the days of Moses, Noah, Jonah and Kind David, but also includes people from the Victorian Age as well as those in the very last days.

We need one hundred and forty-four thousand. We have several of them already. Now you must visit the past and prepare the prophets of the past for their journey into eternal life.

Gabriel's first visit was Moses, who was one hundred and twenty years old. As he lay on his death bed, Gabriel came to him.

"Are you ready for eternal life?" he asked. Moses said nothing but his spirit joined the angel for a trip he knew would be amazing. He had no idea just how amazing it would be.

Gabriel went to visit King David, calling him to follow the Lord in spirit as his body was to die, but first David charged his son, Solomon, become the leader of his people.

Gabriel came to Solomon carrying him on to eternity as his Earthly life came to an end.   He also came to the deathbeds of many others, such as Joseph, Noah, and Abraham. He was there for the departure of John the Baptist, the apostle, Paul, as well as all the Apostles. He needed not to visit Jesus for he was already with the Father.

When he had finished the gathering, he came back to the Master and reported that his job was done.

Chapter 12 (Detectives can be Saved, Too!)

Meanwhile Andorra and Harmony went back to finishing what they had begun with Jack and Audrey. The two did not know the Angels were there, but they would know.

Jack walked into the office at the precinct, humming to himself as he walked up to Audrey. The two were amazingly professional. One would have never thought they had just enjoyed a romantic episode the night before. They simply went about business as normal.

They both believed that Lynn did not hurt Sarah, but he was the last one to be seen with her and they could consider that he may have had a motive—the motive being that she was slow to tell her boyfriend she had found a new lover.

"That's a stretch, though," said Audrey. "I mean we don't really know what went on between them that night and nobody actually saw anything.

"I think we should call him in for another talk," Jack said. "Maybe we can clear him of this and try to find who actually hurt her."

Jack could not figure why he felt so sure that it was not Lynn who had killed the girl. Audrey was at a loss for a reason but they both wanted one. They went back to the crime scene one more time and then each took one side of the street to see if they could find anyone who saw anything.

Audrey came into the bar across the street from the alley where they found Sarah's body.

"I'm Detective Shoemaker," she announced. "Does anyone here remember seeing anything out of the ordinary the night that girl was killed across the street?"

Nobody said anything. There was Arnold nursing a beer. He wanted to speak up, but since he had a rap sheet he was afraid to get involved. He didn't know her, anyway. Somehow he had this strong feeling that he should break with his age old tradition of 'who cares' and tell what he saw that night. He fought against it and Audrey finally left the bar.

It was about quitting time when she and Jack met. Neither had learned anything. One of the frustrations with their job was long hours of disappointing searches without results.

"Let's pick up on this in the morning," offered Jack. "You wanna have dinner with me tonight?"

Audrey accepted and the two of them headed back to their apartments for a shower.

It was about seven when Jack came knocking at Audrey's door. They went to the same restaurant. Neither Jack nor Audrey wanted to talk business right now. They seemed to want to know more about each other.

Audrey shared some of her childhood with Jack. It was a childhood that was not overly happy.

"When I was nine my sister got raped by some bum on the street," she told Jack. "I guess that's why I got into police work. Julia had never hurt anyone. Her only sin was being in the wrong place at the wrong time. This guy came up to her and told her he had lost his dog. She was really naive. He asked her to check out an alley while he looked down another street. He followed her and as soon as she was far enough out of anyone's sight, he raped her."

"Did they ever catch the guy?" asked Jack. Audrey explained that although they did and he did hard time, her sister was never the same. This was not a new concept to Jack. He had seen it many times before.

After they ate, Jack took Audrey back to her apartment. They kissed at the door. Audrey suddenly took the initiative. She wrapped her hand around his neck forcing him closer to her and kissed him with such passion his blood began to boil.

"Would you spend the night with me?" she asked in a husky voice. Who was Jack to refuse.

Around midnight, there pieces of clothing scattered across the floor. There were guns and cufflinks cast aside on the floor as the two slept peacefully in Audrey's bed.

The following morning, the two showered together before they picked everything up, got dressed and headed for the precinct.

Once they were at work, they were the same professional couple they had been.

"Let's see if we can get Lynne to give us a DNA sample," Jack urged. "If we don't find anything we can clear him and more on."

"I don't think that would prove anything," Audrey offered. "Remember, they had spent the night together the night before."

"Still, it may help move us on," Jack insisted. The two went to visit Lynn one more time.

Lynn's reaction was an angry one. He didn't see why they were hounding him. The last time he had seen Sarah, she was alive.

"I told you, I would kill myself before I could hurt Sarah. I'm not going to let you people come around trying to pin this on me."

No matter how much the detectives tried to reason with him, Lynn was angry, hurt and in no mood to be reasoned with.

"We can't get a warrant with no more evidence than we have," said Audrey.

Just then, one of the other officers came up to their desk.

"There's a guy out here who says he may be able to help with the Sarah Fontana case," he said.

"Send him back," instructed Jack. A few minutes later Arnold Moats came walking in.

Jack introduced himself and Audrey and got Arnold's full name. Then he instructed Arnold to have a seat.

"What do you have for us?" Frank asked. Arnold swallowed before he began to explain himself. He still couldn't understand why he suddenly wanted to do this. Something just kept telling him to do something right for a change.

"I didn't see that girl get killed," he began. "I did see her that evening, though. She and this tall fella, about six foot tall with dark hair came out of the hotel across the street from the bar I go to."

"What were you doing when you saw them?" Jack asked.

"Smokin' a cigarette," answered Arnold. "Anyway, I saw them come out of the hotel. They talked for a minute or two and then they kissed and he got into the cab and left. That was when this other fella' came up to her. He seemed really mad. I figured she had been seeing the guy who had just driven off in the cab on the sly or something. Anyway, she gives this guy a slap in the face and walked away around the corner. He stood there for only a few seconds and went running after her. I didn't figure it was any of my business so I went on into the bar for a beer."

"Weren't you in the bar yesterday when I asked about this?" Audrey enquired.

"Yeah," answered Arnold. "I wanted to say something; I've had a couple of run-ins with the police and I didn't want to get involved."

"Why are you here now?" asked Jack. Arnold shrugged. He gazed out the window as he answered.

"I don't know what has come over me; I felt I needed to do the right thing at least once in my life."

"Do you think you'd recognize the second guy if you saw him?" prompted Audrey.

"I think, but I was across the street." He answered.

"You say you were in front of the bar?" Jack asked. Arnold nodded.

"Where were they?" he prompted. "In front of the hotel?"

No, she had walked away after the first guy rode off in the cab. She was in front of the delicatessen about three doors down from the hotel," said Arnold.

"We want you to sit with our sketch artist for a spell," requested Jack. "We need to know what this man looked like."

"I'll give it my best shot," exclaimed Arnold. "Remember, I was across the street."

"Anything you can remember will help," Audrey said by way of encouragement.

Sure enough, the sketch looked like Joe Morton. The two detectives shared a look.

"I think we have enough for a search warrant and an arrest warrant," said Joe. Audrey agreed.

Before long the two, along with some other officers, were knocking on the door at Joe's apartment.

Joe came to the door, gave a sigh and invited the two detectives in.

"I hope you found the guy who did this to Sarah," he breathed. Then he noticed the other officers by their side and went white. Audrey answered by handing him the papers. As the officers cuffed Joe, Audrey read him his rights and Jack proceeded to go over his apartment for anything that might be useful.

By this time Joe was shouting.

"Why is it always the one who is hurt the most that you guys zero in on?" he asked. "I loved Sarah. Why would I hurt her?"

"Maybe you loved her too much," said Jack.

"Or maybe you didn't love her enough," suggested Audrey. The officers escorted Joe out and the two detectives and others in the crime squad went through Joe's apartment, looking for clues.

After a time of going through everything and finding nothing, one of the detectives called Jack and Audrey to the closet.

"Well, will you look at that?" he asked in a tone that was more an exclamation than a question.

"The treads on these shoes are a perfect match to the footprints one of the crime lab workers found at the murder scene."

"Could be a coincidence," uttered Jack. Audrey turned to walk away and stopped in her tracks when the officers answered.

"Not likely," he began. "See the red stuff on the outer curve of the soul? It matches the photo taken at the crime scene."

"What is it?" asked Audrey, stretching her neck for a closer look.

"If I'm right, when we take these downtown we will find they are cranberries," answered the officer. This caused them all to start laughing.

"Cranberries?" echoed Audrey. "How did cranberries get on his shoes?"

"Remember, we found the girls body next to a dumpster. I couldn't be sure how, but it's a good bet that some of them spilled while they were emptying the dumpster." As he spoke he carefully put the shoes into a plastic to take them downtown for further analysis.

"Maybe we should go back to the crime scene," Audrey said.

"Probably not going to find anything now. They have probably cleaned that alley a couple of times since the murder," said the officer. "There is one more thing, though.

"What's that?" Jack chirped. "You'll find some Thanksgiving turkey?"

"Very funny," replied the officer with more than a hint of sarcasm. "Did you notice that on the other side of the sole of the shoe there was leftover asphalt. They had just patched a pothole and it was evidently still fresh when he stepped into it. You can see it here," he said while pulling out the photo that had been taken at the crime scene.

"We'll be able to tell for sure once we get this downtown." They were soon on their way downtown.

The next morning the lab called with the results. Sure enough, it was cranberries on the soles of Joe's shoes and likewise it was fresh asphalt.

From this point on, the detectives knew they would have little trouble making a case against Joe Morton.

Chapter 13 (Back To the Future)

At this point, Andorra and Harmony were called by the Master. A very important moment in history was about to occur. They needed to be with Arty and with George, Frank, Allison, Stew and a host of others.

These were to be the first of one hundred and forty-four thousand who had been picked in order to begin the harvest of chosen ones.

Frank was in the middle of a transmission with Earth, when the signal was lost.

On Earth, there was panic. One of the officials tried calming the people.

"After all," he began. "We lost Frank once for a couple of seconds. We'll get them back."

Several seconds passed and then several minutes without contact. Now even he was getting worried.

After three days, they started to scramble spacecraft. John Holt was the official's name, and now he was genuinely concerned.

"Let's move up launch dates for the next three shuttles," he instructed. He wanted to know why they had lost contact. He had no idea what they would do. It took almost seven months to get a shuttle to the space station. He could only hope this was a radio problem and everyone onboard the space station was okay.

Actually, they were in better shape than ever but not in the way John had hoped for.

At the very moment when radio contact was lost, Arty, Andorra, Harmony, Gabriel and a host of other angels became visible not only to the person they were assigned to, but they were also visible to each person onboard.

Nobody felt even an ounce of panic. This was the most wonderful and fulfilling moment any of them had ever felt.

They all took turns introducing themselves to one another. Among them was King David, Solomon, Noah, Moses, Jonah, and more—everyone Gabriel had visited from the past.

Then they all heard the voice of the Master. His voice seemed to surround them all and he began to explain that they were the beginning of the great harvest.

There was a mixture of excitement, bafflement and maybe a little nervousness for some, although Moses, Jonah, King David and the others knew what was happening. However, this was bigger than even they had thought it would be.

There was another strange thing about this conversation. They were from many different countries and many different times in history so it stood to reason that they each spoke in different languages, yet they each understood the others perfectly.

"The year is twenty-two thousand and thirty five years A.D. There will be no twenty-two thousand thirty six," the Master proclaimed. "My work on Earth is finished.

"What will become of those on the planet Earth?" asked Andorra. She knew of the Master's forgiveness. There was hope that it would extend further.

"Many of them will be given one last chance to turn to me," the Master answered. "That is the job of each of you. I want you to blend in with whatever part of the Earth's past you are sent to. Moses, you will have to change your demeanor. That goes for many of you. Arty, Andorra, Harmony, Frank, Allison, George and Gabriel are to finish what they have started. The rest of you will give those on Earth one last chance to turn from their sinful ways."

"If they don't, what then?" asked Arty. The Master dismissed it with a simple statement upon which he would not elaborate.

"You need not be concerned about that," he said flatly. "First, I want to show your new friends where their new bodies will find home."

Suddenly the space station and the black void of space were replaced by the most beautiful blue sky and a wonderfully kept garden with fruits and vegetables growing on trees and bushes everywhere they looked.

"I said Adam and Eve were driven out of the Garden of Eden," mused the Master. "I did not destroy it. It will be your new home and the home of many others whose eternal lives will be saved through your works. You have all become Angels of God!"

George, Allison, Frank and all those who had been on the spacecraft were amazed and befuddled.

"Wow!" exclaimed Allison. Frank simply stood silently and enjoyed the beauty of the place where they stood.

"Where are we?" asked Arty. He was a little slow in taking all this in, even though he had been an angel for quite some time.

"This is a planet in a universe that the people on Earth could never reach. You would not be here as flesh and blood," said the Master. "This is Heaven!"

The Master's voice was heard by all, though nobody saw him. There were a few points he wanted to make before sending them on the task of harvesting.

"Arty," he began. "Do you know why you are here?" Arty was at a loss for words so he simply shook his head.

"You are here because my love for you is greater than your past sins," the Master explained.

A voice from the crowd was heard by all. They each turned to look at the one who spoke.

"I am known to those who read the Bible as 'the apostle Paul'." I am here because you saw fit to make a blind man see. I am grateful that forgave me and let me make payment for my sins while still a mortal. Truly, I hated the followers of your son Jesus Christ. How was I to know that you would make me one of them?"

"This is all part of my plan," the Master answered. "Now, I want you each to go back and finish the harvesting of lost souls. There will be much rejoicing here in my kingdom over every soul that is saved.

"All those who were on the space station stay here for a debriefing. The others are instructed to go back and finish your work."

With that, Andorra and Harmony found themselves standing in the shadows watching Jack & Audrey work.

Chapter 14(Closing the Case)

"The report came in from the lab," announced Audrey. "Unless someone else was wearing Joe Morton's shoes he was at the crime scene."

"Let's bring him in," suggested Frank. "Oh, and call the D.A.," he added. "I think we have enough to make a case.

When Joe Morton and his attorney entered the interrogation room, they immediately placed him under arrest, read him his rights and then began telling Joe and his attorney Jake Malloy what they had found.

"You have no proof that he was there. We can make a case that he found her there afterward, panicked and ran away," retorted Jake.

"No!" interrupted Joe. "I killed her." His attorney tried to quiet him, but Joe had had enough.

"Look, man," he began. "I killed the only woman I will ever love. What do I have to live for?"

"We're listening," said Audrey. In spite of his attorney's attempts to get Joe to be quiet, he went on to explain what happened.

"I lost my temper," he began. "I truly didn't mean to kill her; I let my own selfishness carry me away. She loved someone else and I couldn't stand the thought of her being with someone else. I didn't handle it well. Instead of telling her of my love, I called her a whore right there on the street. She slapped me and went around the corner. I was so angry I wasn't even thinking. I followed her and when I grabbed her by the arm she pulled away. I wanted to beg her not to leave me. I wanted to tell her I could be better, but she said she had found someone who she could love and she was tired of me and my self-centered attitude. When she turned to walk away I grabbed her again. She slapped me again and I hit her. God help me I hit her," Joe cried out as he put his head on the table.

"Can we get manslaughter?" asked Jake.

Jack shrugged. Audrey watched silently as Joe sat crying into his hands. Jack got up and walked over to the window.

"That's up to the D.A." he answered. "I'd say he probably would entertain a plea; I'm sure it would include life in prison."

Joe was silent, although his attorney kept trying to negotiate. This was not a decision for the officers to make, but he hoped that a good word from them would help. After much discussion Jack announced that he would tell the D.A. that the man's sorrow was genuine and he never meant to hurt Sarah, but that was as far as Jack could go with a clear conscience.

They took the suspect through the entire booking procedure and soon it was time to go home.

As they drove along, Jack suddenly asked Audrey to marry him. She was more than a little taken by surprise. The words just came bursting out of his mouth.

Jack went on to explain that they made a great team. He now knew she was a wonderful partner. He also had figured out that they were soul mates.

"Marry me!" He spoke again with a firmer sound. "Let's not lose this. You're too good for me and I can be good for you, too."

It was a month later when the two said 'I do,' and the chief was Jack's best man.

"Somehow, I knew that lady was just what you needed," he bragged. Jack could only smile.

"So, where are you going on your honeymoon?" asked the chief.

"I'm going to take Audrey to the little town I grew up in," answered Jack.

"I can't thank you enough. You're a good man, Chief."

"Call me Ed," said the Chief.

"Sounds kinda unprofessional, doesn't it?" asked Jack

"For Pete's sake, Jack, said the Chief. "I was the best man at your wedding. Doesn't that make us friends?"   Jack shrugged.

"Yes, I guess it does," he affirmed. "I thought Audrey would like to see where I lived my childhood. I'm not sure it will be the same as when I left it but I would like to stop by, lay some flowers on Mom and Dad's grave and show her the Commons.

"The what?" asked the chief.

"That's what my folks called it," Jack went on. "I was raised in a little town in Western Maryland, about seventy miles away from D.C. The commons was a park where we spent many a summer day."

"I wonder why they called it the commons?" Ed sighed.

"Don't know," answered Jack, "but, we spent many a happy hours there, though we called it the ball park. I was never good enough to make the little league teams, but a bunch of us got together and played ball just about every afternoon during the summer. We played high fence over," he lamented.

"What's high fence over?" asked Ed.

"We didn't have enough players for two nine player teams so we ran the bases backwards. Third base became first base and since the fence down the left field line was a very short distance. The Independent league players didn't want to make a homerun to easy to hit, so they put up a fourteen foot fence that ran almost to center field, where the fence was much further away from home plate. The fence gave us a place to narrow the field so we could play with four or five people on a team," Jack explained.

"The town was founded in 1767," Jack went on. "It was founded by a man name Funck—he named it Jerusalem, I think, in about 1767. The town became incorporated as Funkstown in 1840."

"It sounds like an interesting place to grow up in," said Ed. Jack smiled.

"There's a lot of history there," said Jack. "During the civil war there was a battle fought on the east edge of town as General Lee's troops retreated after the big battle at Gettysburg, Pennsylvania. We used to drive down to the Anita Battle fields quite a lot. We would visit Gettysburg a lot, too," Jack reminisced.

Soon Jack and Audrey were on the road to his home town.

Chapter 15 (Back to the Past)

"So what's this home town of yours like?" asked Audrey. As he drove, Jack explained that he wasn't sure it would be the same.

"When I was a kid there were two grocery stores in town but the last time I went there they were closed and antique shops were everywhere," he said. "They built a memorial on the old route 40. It was a bit so they could have wider road access, I guess. Any way, it used to sit along the right side of the road as you headed into town. Now it's still there but on the left side. Who knows what other changes they made. The town might have grown into something big, but when they put the railroad through, they went through Hagerstown and the inns and mills in Funkstown were shut down. You know, my Dad took us to where there used to be an amusement park but it had been long since shut down."

"Sounds fascinating," said Audrey.

When they got there, Jack realized that the changes were still taking place all around Funkstown but the residents had somehow maintained the historic value of the town.

They found a Motor Inn in Hagerstown to stay since they found none in Funkstown, itself.

Audrey was curious about this quaint little town. She asked questions and listened as Jack tried as best he could to give answers.

"We learned in school that Funkstown or Jerusalem started out as a plot of eighty-eight acres of land that was sold to a German immigrant named Henry

Funck in 1754. The town was laid out by Henry and his brother, Jacob, in 1767, in think," Jack began. "The town is surrounded on three sides by the Antietam Creek. That's why there were so many mills."

"What kind of mills?" asked Audrey.

"Various kinds," said Jack. "There was a powder mill that supplied Washington's army during the Revolutionary war. The largest of them all was a flour mill that Funck himself built in 1762. That was near where the fire hall is now. I was told they never rebuilt after it was destroyed by a fire. The powder mill blew up in 1810."

"That's a lot of history," sighed Audrey. "It's such a beautiful little town. I hope they never lose the wonderful atmosphere."

"My dad told me about an electric trolley in which he and his father rode. It ran from Hagerstown, through Funkstown, Boonsboro, and ended up in Frederick, about twenty-nine miles away. Some time in the middle of the century it went out of business. I don't know but I imagine that's what happened to the amusement park." Jack smiled as he reached for Audrey.

"Maybe tomorrow, I'll take you to Boonsboro. You know the old route 40 was once the only road that led to Boonsboro, Middletown and Frederick."

"I'd love to see it," Audrey said emphatically. Audrey had been raised in the city. The rural area was a wonderful treat. As a kid her dad would take the family on trips in the summer. They would usually find some mountain area in the upper part of New York State, but rarely did they ever get further south than

New Jersey. This and the fact that she was with the man she loved was enough to keep her more than happy.

"Jack," she asked as they sat eating at the restaurant in the motor inn, "when did you say the memorial was built?"

Jack took a bite of food and after wiping his mouth, he took a breath, trying to remember.

"I think some guy named Weisner started building it. I think he finished it in 1921. They said that was the main square but by the time I came along the square was considered to be a block north."

"We used to visit the Antietam Battlefield which isn't far out of town regularly," Jack Lamented. "Of course, the trip of all trips was when we went on a long drive into Virginia. Dad would take us to Skyline Drive every fall. You have never seen anything so beautiful as the Virginia Mountains when the fall airs starts to turn the leaves so many beautiful colors."

"I'd love to see it," said Audrey. "Maybe we could come back down this way in the fall and make that part of our trip."

"At this moment, I have something else in mind," Jack said with a husky sound to his voice.

"Are you ready to go up to our room?" Audrey asked, although she already knew the answer.

The two spent the night sweating up the sheets as they made love like never before. The would take spells to rest, holding each other close and caressing one another but before long, they would become impassioned again and the walls would ring with their moaning sounds.

The next morning they drove to Boonsboro and over the mountain past an Inn where Jack had eaten many times as a child. They eventually ended at Frederick where they simply road around before heading back.

On the way back to Hagerstown, they stopped at the Inn on top of the mountain and had dinner.

As they ate the two made conversation. Audrey was curious as to what else was in the town besides antique shops and grocery stores.

"We had one barber shop," Jack answered. "And a lady moved into town and opened a home based business called *The Doll Shop*. She would take old antique dolls, repair and dress them up and sell them. Before long people were bringing their old dolls for her to fix. From what I could tell her business was flourishing. I think she's still in business."

"I'd really like to see that," said Audrey. Jack offered to drop by before they went back to the motor inn. This was never to come to be.

Then, there came the ironic twist of events that ended with their car going off the road and into the water of the Antietam Creek.

Ed was working as usual when his phone rang. He picked it up. An old friend of his had decided several years ago to get out of the city life and move to a more rural location. He was now working for the sheriffs department of Washington County, Maryland. He had some very bad news for Ed.

The car Jack was driving went off the road at the place commonly known in the area as Death Curve and ended up in the Antietam Creek with Jack and Audrey in it.

"Are they alright?" Ed asked before his friend could go further. He listened carefully but there was a long silence on the other end. When it was finally broken his friend simply said,

"I'm sorry. They didn't make it." Ed sat staring out the window. He would have about halfway expected it if some fool shot Jack in the line of duty but to have him and Audrey meet their death on their honeymoon? This he could not comprehend.

"God, how could you let this happen?" he charged. "How could you take their lives today of all days?"

Ed felt the pain deeper than he ever felt he could. He was looking forward to the possibility of Jack and Audrey maybe one day having kids. He could be their Godfather.

He had just grown close to the couple and they were snuffed away from him.

As Ed grieved, someone else was receiving a call. Beatrice Edmonson picked up her phone and was told of the death of her twin sister and her new brother-in-law.

Bee, as everyone called her, didn't make the wedding. Now she hated herself for letting business get in the way. She would have seen her sister one last time. What really made her feel bad is the fact that they were identical twins but had grown apart over the last eight or nine years. She had her life and Audrey had hers. That seemed to be the way they each wanted it. Now, however, she was wishing they had spent more time together.

After hanging up the phone she went into the bedroom and dragged out the old family album that she had not often bothered to look at in the past few years until now. Suddenly, it was all that was left of Audrey, and Bee felt the need to contemplate.

Ed and Bee did not even know each other but they did share something in common. For the next three days they would both mourn the loss of loved ones.

Three days later, Ed pulled into the parking lot of the Funeral home to attend the viewing. When he walked in he saw the two caskets sitting side by side in front. In front of one was a woman. Ed stared at her unbelievingly.

"Audrey?" he almost spurted out but stopped himself. It couldn't be her. He wished it were but he knew it couldn't be.

"My name is Beatrice Edmonson," she announced. "I was Audrey's twin sister—am Audrey's twin sister," she amended as an afterthought.

"I didn't know she had one," Ed wondered. "Oh," he said after a brief moment of thought. "I'm sorry. I'm Ed Wingert. I didn't realize Audrey had any living relatives. She didn't speak about her personal life much."

"We hadn't been real close over the past couple of years," said Bee. "I regret that now. If only I could go back and relive those last couple of years I would change that. It's too late now."

She returned her gaze to the lifeless body of her sister. They didn't say much more after that.

The funeral was painful but Ed tried to control his sorrow. One thing that lightened the load some for him was the beautiful lady sitting in the front. Ed couldn't keep himself from glancing over at Bee. It was as if Audrey had come back from the dead. At one point, she saw him looking and managed a weak smile and then turned her attention back to the coffin where her dead sister lay.

When it was all over, Ed took the rest of the day off. He went home to his apartment. Jack and Audrey had become his best friends. Ed had not allowed himself anything in the way of friendship until now. He contemplated this. How ironic it was. The first time he allowed himself to care about someone on a personal level, they were stripped away from him. This pain he didn't want. Maybe that was why he never allowed himself to be made vulnerable until now. He decided he would not let this happen again. He was not going to open himself up to pain again.

"You're taking on a rather cynical attitude, there, my friend." This was a voice he knew well. Ed turned and there sat Jack.

Ed wasn't sure what was happening to himself, now. He swore he was losing his mind.

"No, you are not crazy," Jack answered his unspoken question. "I am real. Well, as real as I can be to you. There is something about my death that you don't completely understand. That is why the Master has instructed me to make you the first person on my 'to do' list.

Chapter 16(Yes, Ed. There is a God)

"Master," Ed questioned? "To do list?" he added. "I think you're just a hallucination. I would love for you to be alive but they just buried you. I think I need counseling of some kind."

"Okay," Jack answered. "I'll be your counselor. Let me tell you what our honeymoon was like." Ed just sat and listened. He wasn't sure what was happening to him, but he was beginning to doubt his sanity.

"I took Audrey back to my hometown and we had a wonderful time. We visited all the old places where I played as a kid and Audrey loved hearing me go on and on about the great times I had," he continued.

"We Drove down to Boonsboro, Maryland. It's just a little south of the town I grew up in. When we were coming home, Audrey was talking some about her childhood and a voice from the back of the car interrupted her." Jack went on to explain that as Audrey was telling about some of the games that she and her sister, who she called Honeybee or Bee for short, had played, Arty piped up and exclaimed.

"Man, I never really had a childhood. I hope you two know how lucky you are."

Jack explained how he almost ran the car off the road right there but managed to keep his composure.

"Who are you?" he inquired. "And how did you get into the car? We were doing fifty miles an hour."

"Oh, I can do better than that," Arty Answered. "I am here because the Master wants to save the two of you. Come with me and you will have an adventure you have never dreamed was possible. Believe me, it will be worth it. It sure has been for me."

Jack went on to tell Ed how Arty explained his childhood, his relationship with Andora and his untimely death. Only, it was more like walking into a wonderful life and Arty had explained that he knew he did not deserve it.

"I guess it was a gift," he praised the Master.

"Who is this Master?" Jack enquired.

"God!" Arty stated emphatically. God is my Master. He is the source of all life and anyone who knows him through his son Jesus has a doorway to eternal life. Funny thing is I didn't even know I knew him till after we went over that cliff in the buggy. In fact, I didn't know him until about a hundred years or so afterward.

"I don't get it," said Jack emphatically. "Why are you here?" Arty turned and gazed out the car window. He was enjoying the beauty of the spring flowers and newly budding trees. Then he stopped his contemplation long enough to answer Jack.

"I'm a reaper, he said." Jack looked off the road long enough to study Arty through the rear view mirror.

"A what?" he asked.

"I am what you might call a gatherer. I am an Angel of God. I am sent to reap souls for the Kingdom."

"Are you here for us?" asked Audrey, who had been extremely quiet until now. "I don't think we are ready to go now. We both want to have kids. We haven't lived our lives together yet."

"It's your time," Arty quipped. "The Master said today is your day." Audrey turned and stared into the eyes of the Angel in the back seat.

"That hardly seems fair," she cried out. "Ask the Master if he couldn't give us some time together before he takes us. This is our honeymoon."

"Sweetheart, you are going to have eternity together," Arty consoled. "Isn't that what you want?"

Audrey fell silent for a spell. Then she turned to Arty again. Her eyes implored him. She couldn't understand why God felt that shortening their lives was the right thing.

"We had plans," she began. Then, as if she needed something specific she told him that Jack had promised to show her Skyline Drive.

"Oh, we can do that Arty said. Then he placed a hand on each of their shoulders and they suddenly were not in the car anymore. They were floating far above it. Jack and Audrey watched as the car came upon "Death Curve." It did not turn but ran off the road into the water below.

Now, they were both silent. Arty was still holding them.

"All of a sudden," Jack began. "I didn't feel worry or trouble or anything negative. I felt more at home than I had ever felt in my life. I should have been scared. After all, we were about sixty feet off the ground.

"What happened next," Ed asked. Suddenly, he felt the presence of the Master, though he didn't know why. He was never a religious person but this was a wonderful joy.

"What happened next was Arty took us on our first trip through time," laughed Jack. "True to his word, he said he wanted to show Audrey Skyline Drive. Audrey said it was useless. She wanted to see it in the fall when the leaves turn the beautiful array of colors but Arty told her we were going to the fall. She didn't understand what he was talking about until the area on Alternate Forty faded and we were standing at an overlook on Skyline Drive. The colors were more gorgeous than I had remembered. I asked him how this was possible. Arty said, "With Angels of the Master all things are possible."

'We can travel through time just like you used to walk from one room to another in the flesh," he told me. "You will see more than you ever could see as a man.'

Then he took us to the Heavens. It was beautiful. I couldn't find the words to describe it to you. One day, you will see it too. The Master has already saved a place for you in Heaven, Ed. First, though, you must work out some issues here on Earth."

"What issues?" Ed asked incredulously. He was suddenly feeling very nervous. Jack picked up on that nervousness and tried to console him.

"Listen," he began. "I didn't get a chance to finish working with Joe Morton. I need you to do something for me."

"Joe Morton is in jail," Ed retorted. "You have nothing more to do." Jack smiled and explained that he wanted Ed to visit the man in jail.

"He will try to kill himself," he said. Ed answered that he probably deserved to die for what he did.

"Listen, man," Jack replied. "The man did something in anger and now he feels a remorse that he will carry for the rest of his life. Actually, life in prison is a harsher penalty than death. As long as he lives, he will feel the remorse. You need to give him comfort."

"You're an Angel," said Ed. "You certainly don't need me. Go and sprinkle some fairy dust on him or something."

Jack smiled again. He knew Ed would fight this. Ed had been working with people who committed these violent crimes for years. He had become very negative. Jack knew the feeling. He had been, too. It was when he met Audrey that he began to see that someone must have been looking after him. It was her love that had expanded his mind. The problem was that he could not explain to Ed why he wanted his help. It was not that Jack needed it. It was that Ed did. His eternal salvation would hinge on his ability to take on a more forgiving attitude. Jack would have liked to explain to Ed that Sarah, the woman Joe had killed, was alive and well in a place where pain had no place. This, he would have to let Ed figure out on his own. He simply moved on.

"You are going to go to sleep now," he began. "When you awaken, it will be as if all this were a dream. But I will be working with you from the shadows. You must visit this man and get to know him.

"I still don't understand," Ed protested.

What Jack had learned while in the Heavenly city was that anything Ed did with the purpose of saving his own soul or claiming eternal life would not count. He needed to do his good deeds because of love. His eternal salvation was dependant upon his ability to simply place the love of his fellow man above his own life. The Son of God once said, "He who would save his life, must lose it. He that loses his life for my sake, the same shall be saved."

This was why it was important for Jack to have his help. It was not for the sake of Joe so much as it was for Ed's sake.

"I saw something about the man," Jack explained. "He is carrying a heavy load. He did not mean to hurt that girl. He simply lost his temper and exploded. Now, he is considering taking his own life. He is in prison. The one person on the face of the earth is dead and he is the one who killed her. In his heart he is not even blaming her for her affair with another man. He is taking it all upon himself. Somebody must help him."

"But, why me?" Ed complained. "I helped put him in jail and he confessed to killing her."

"Maybe that's why you," Ed retorted. "Maybe he needs to hear someone who was involved with the whole thing say they understand. You are his earthly angel, Chief."

"Ed," his boss interrupted.

"Ed," said Jack. "You are Joe's earthly angel. How would you feel if you were responsible for the death of the person you love?"

Ed's eyes began to mist. He sat for several moments contemplating what Jack had just said. Then he sighed.

"There but by the grace of God, go I," he breathed softly. Jack smiled.

"Exactly!" he responded.

"O.K., I'll stop by in the morning and visit this guy," Ed agreed. "The least I can do is, see his frame of mind."

With those words, his eyes grew heavy and he went to sleep right there on the chair. He awoke sometime later. Somehow, he wasn't sure if Jack's visit had been a dream or not. By morning he felt it was a dream, but he still felt compelled to visit Joe and see what was happening with him.

Chapter 16 (Bee, There is More to Life than You Ever Knew)

While Jack was with Ed, Audrey was called by the Master to visit her sister. Bee went into the house after the funeral. She was wiping tears from her eyes; no matter how many times she wiped them away, her face was streaked with tears. She wished she would have been able to talk to Audrey one last time.

Alas, she had not called her sister, not even to say she could not make her wedding. Instead, she attended Audrey's funeral.

Bee knew her face had to be a mess. Tears and makeup do not make for a beautiful complexion. She walked into the bathroom, switched on the light and looked in the mirror at her tear-soaked face.

As she stared, her mind contemplated why she and Audrey had grown apart. It was as much sibling rivalry as anything. Their mom and dad—who were now passed away—had been super proud of Audrey. Bee felt like they did not have much pride in her and that caused her to feel a resentment she now regretted.

That was when she noticed the complexion on the reflection in the mirror changing. The streaks were gone and the face looking back at her was smiling although she wasn't smiling.

Her hand reflexively rose to her cheek but the reflection simply looked back at her, smiling.

This freaked Bee out and she turned and stumbled into the living room. She was sure she was going crazy.

"I'm sorry," the words came a voice from behind her. Bee turned to see Audrey sitting on the sofa.

"I couldn't resist the temptation," chuckled Audrey. Bee was still in shock and said nothing.

"Listen," Audrey began. "I was sent here by the Master to give you closure. After all, you were not the only one who didn't bother to visit her sister. I could have come to see you. I just never did."

Bee finally took a breath and managed to speak. She couldn't fathom why Audrey was here. She was in a box six feet under ground at the cemetery.

"My body is there," Audrey explained. "My Spirit is anywhere the Master asks me to go. The first thing he wanted me to do was relieve myself of the guilt of a horrible transgression. I should have come to see you, but I didn't"

"I should have come to see you," said Bee. "But, I was jealous of you. Mom and Dad were so proud of you. I don't think I could ever live up to their expectations and you did. I wish I had been more proud of you and thought a little less about my hurt feelings."

It was then that Audrey cut her off with an admission that took her breath away. She raised her hand to shush her sister and then she breathed a statement which she had never admitted until now.

"I flaunted that at you," she proclaimed. "I should have been a source of comfort to you; instead I chose to enjoy my feeling of superiority. I am sorry, Honeybee. I was selfish and completely ignorant to treat you like that." Then she sighed heavily and added.

"It's sad that I would only understand this now. We could have had some wonderful times together."

There were tears welling up in Bee's eyes. She couldn't remember when Audrey called her *Honeybee* last. It was a term of endearment that she had used a lot while they were growing up.

Then Audrey smiled and reached out to hug Bee. She had forgotten that she couldn't touch, and Bee almost walked into the wall as she passed through the image of her sister.

"Oh, sorry," Audrey apologized. "I forgot. I don't have a body any more. Try to remember something for me, Honeybee. Always know that as sure as there is a God I will be with you always, just as Jesus will be with you always."

Then she faded away and Bee sat down in the chair. As she contemplated what had just happened she fell asleep. When she awoke, it was as if she had dreamed the whole thing, but there was a feeling of peace that she thought she would never feel again.

Bee got ready to go to work. Before she left the house she looked up Ed's phone number and wrote it down on a note pad. Tearing the page off, she put it into her purse.

The first opportunity she got at work, she took a break and phoned him. When she got the answering machine she told him who she was and asked if they could get together. Bee felt a little self-conscience about calling a man that she had only met once, but he knew Audrey and she needed to vent. She could feel Ed's pain over the loss of his friends, so she took a deep breath and began talking.

"Hello, Mr. Wingert," she began. "This is Beatrice Edmonson. If you have a chance, I need to talk to you. I really don't have anyone else and I am feeling the loss of my sister and your friend to be a heavy cross to bear."

She also gave her phone number and hung up. She wasn't sure Ed would reply but something told her to try.

As it turned out, Ed would not get home until late that evening; true to his word he took a long lunch break and went to visit Joe at the prison.

The guards did not cut Ed any slack. They made him go through the same routine that any visitor to the prison had to endure. After he left his gun and anything else that would set off the metal detectors in a locker, Ed walked through. When it did not let out the shrill sound, he had his hand stamped and a wrist band placed around his left wrist. Then he sat down and waited. Soon Joe's name was announced through the loud speaker and Ed got up and went through the first gate, waited on it to close and the second gate to open and then walked into the next building where Joe sat.

Joe had been on suicide watch and was not allowed in the visiting room, itself. He was in a booth with a Plexiglas window and a telephone.

When he saw that it was Ed, his face dropped. After a moment of silence in which both tried to find some words without success, it was Ed who finally said something.

"I thought I would stop by and see how you are doing," he said. Even as he heard himself saying it, Ed could not help but feel rather lame.

From the look on Joe's face, Ed expected something like, "how do you think I am? I'm in prison." Instead Joe studied Ed's eyes for a moment and then his look softened somewhat.

"I'm here," he said. Somehow he could not come right out and say what he was feeling. He hated himself for what he had done. What made matters worse for him was the fact that he had time to think about why Sarah had been seeing that other guy. Deep down, inside, Joe knew he had driven her to do it.

"Listen," Ed began. "This is a little awkward. I promised Jack I would stop by and see how you were doing. He said he felt you were really sorry for what happened and he wanted to help you deal with the sorrow."

"I'm dealing with it," Joe said flatly. "If Jack cared so much, why isn't he here?"

Ed sighed as his eyes dropped down. Joe couldn't tell what he was saying, but the despair that showed on Ed's face made him nervous. Finally Ed broke the thirty-seconds of silence.

"He's dead," he said. He and Audrey were on their honeymoon. The car went off the road and they were both pronounced dead at the scene."

"Bummer." It was a weak response but it was all Joe could say at first. Then after a few breaths he looked from Ed's eyes and gazed at his free hand, clinched on the table between him and his visitor. "If God wanted to take someone, he should have taken me. I deserve to die. I killed the only person on Earth that I could ever love."

"It's hard to think like God," Ed exclaimed. Now he was lost in thought. He was staring but not focusing on anything.

"I take it, you've tried," answered Joe.

"Not until now," said Ed. "Now, I am trying to figure this creator out for the first time in my life and it took the death of a friend to make me do it." He wanted to tell Joe about his visit with Jack but he was sure Joe would think he was crazy or simply hallucinating out of grief, so he kept it to himself.

"Well, if you do figure him out, let me know. I would like to ask him some questions," Joe retorted with a hint of skepticism in his voice.

Suddenly, without knowing why, Ed felt empowered. He didn't know where this insight was coming from, but he felt a need to comfort a man he hardly knew other than the man he had helped convict of a murder.

"What would you ask him?" He enquired. "More importantly, what would you tell him?" Ed didn't even understand where that last sentence came from but he would, eventually.

"I would ask him why I was so blind for all those years and I would tell him I was sorry."

"Sorry for what?" Ed prompted.

Joe's eyes dropped down again. As he stared at the palm of his free hand he took a deep breath and then spoke softly into the phone.

"I drove her away," he started. "She wanted me to be romantic and loving and for a while I was. She wanted kids but I didn't want the responsibility. She wanted me to love her like she loved me and I did, but I simply didn't show it. I became caught up in my job. I was working long hours and when I came home I was tired. I wouldn't even notice the romantic way she hinted at her desires, even when it included wearing scanty night clothes. I had become completely dysfunctional. After a couple of years of trying, she simply gave up on me and went looking for someone who could make her feel loved."

Joe was crying now. Tears were running down his face. He reached into his pocket for a tissue and wiped his face.

"I got angry and pushed her. I didn't mean to kill her but I was blaming her for what she had done to me. All along, it was me who had done it to her. I was too dumb to know what I wanted. I should have wanted kids. I should have wanted to hold her in my arms. I should have loved her but I chose to become a sexless tyrant."

Now there were tears beginning to well up in Ed's eyes. He looked at the man on the other side of the glass with a brand new point of view.

"One moment of insanity and you pay for it for the rest of your life," Joe sighed. "You don't know how close I have come to killing myself. I should have done that before I hurt Sarah."

"Sarah is Gods hands now," said Ed. He wondered where that kind of talk was coming from. It didn't sound like the kind of thing he would say or even think.

"Listen," he continued. "Maybe there are others in here who you can help. Maybe there are a lot of people who need to find their peace with God. Maybe it takes a lot of heartache to make a man, I don't know. I do know that you are a good man. If I could, I would get you out of there. Unfortunately, the laws of this state are not forgiving, but God is. Ask him how you can make amends."

After a few more minutes of talk, the guard came up and announced that their time was up. Ed got up and left but not before he promised he would return and visit Joe again.

Ed found his frame of mind was changed. He looked at the cases that floated past his desk with a completely different attitude. He wasn't looking for convictions as much as he wondered what caused the people to do what he knew some of them did. Others, he wondered if they were even guilty at all.

He got through the day with much soul searching and after stopping at a restaurant he headed home.

When he got there he pushed the button and there was Bee's voice repeating the message she had left earlier in the day.

Chapter 17 (Woe to the World)

In the year two-thousand, three hundred years there were three shuttles heading for the space station. Everyone was intent on finding out what happened that cut off communication three years before. The shuttles were nearing the space station. John Borden and his crew were in one shuttle. Lizzy Jenkins and her crew in the second and Adam Shoemaker and crew were in the third. Calculation had them about six months from the space station. They still had heard nothing from the space station.

John, Lizzy and Adam were in constant contact with Earth and with each other. They kept hoping someone was picking up something. This hope was ill-founded, though. If Earth had picked up on the transmission, they would have surely received it too.

Lizzy was short for Elizabeth. It was a term of endearment that her mother had given her as a kid and it never grew old.

Every day was the same. They were constantly sending reports back from Earth and hoping for some insight that they were not in a position to get from so far into outer space. They took turns sleeping. Just as the crew on Earth, there was someone monitoring every statistic which was a combination of information which they sent back to earth and the Earth's radar findings.

One day in the middle of the transmission while John, Lizzy and Adam were going through the grill, there came an interruption.

"We're under attack," yelled the voice from Earth. The three astronauts tried to find out what was going on, but suddenly there was no sound from Earth at all. They were cut off.

They began to panic. Was it this that had happened to Frank and the others on board the space station?

"I doubt it is," said Adam. "This time it seems to be the Earth that is cut off." They continued to listen for something, anything that would ease their minds, but there was no more communication with the Earth.

Lizzy finally came to a horrible realization. She knew the inevitable had come. She wasn't sure but she was haunted by a picture of what had probably cut them off with the Earth forever.

"They've finally done it," she said with some anger in her voice. "They've been fighting with each other for centuries. It was only a matter of time before they destroyed themselves."

John wanted to say he didn't think so, but he felt that she was probably right. Adam, likewise contemplated what he thought was probably the sad truth. They had engaged in war on Earth and it could only mean devastation.

The three of them had watched as the nations of the Earth made one last attempt at living peacefully together. They had even elected a world council to police the various countries and keep them in line with the good of all. In spite of this, there were many countries that conspired to take control. They resented the council and wanted to create their own laws. Among other things they did not want were the rules of how to monitor nuclear capabilities. Nuclear power was widely used. In fact, there were few countries that did not have their own nuclear power plants.

"I could see this coming," said Lizzy. "I knew it was only a matter of time." John and Adam said nothing. Finally John did speak.

"Well, if we can't go back to Earth and we have no idea what is ahead at the space station, what do we do?" he asked.

It was Adam who answered this question.

"We go find out what's ahead," he said. "If we can't live on the space station, maybe we can find a planet somewhere out here that will sustain life. It's our only hope."

"We'll be out of oxygen before we find one," groaned Lizzy. "There isn't another planet for millions of miles and perhaps not even further. There's probably not a planet that will sustain life even if we had the ability to get to it. Everything is void."

Lizzy had carried an old Bible that had been handed down from generation to generation. Nobody believed it was more than ancient literature by now, but she carried it because her mother had it by her bedside. Her mother had it there because her mother gave it to her and it was a gift from her mother.

Suddenly Lizzy wanted to read it. She didn't know why, but she might have been looking for some kind of comfort. At this point the future looked even more dismal than it had for all her life.

Lizzy sat quietly and opened the Bible to the place where her mother had left a bookmark. Her eyes fell upon the teachings of Jesus Christ. It read:

"And Jesus answered and said unto them, take heed that no man deceive you. For many shall come in my name, saying, I am Christ and shall deceive many."

Lizzy remembered her father telling her about the people who came saying they were the Christ. The government finally passed a law prohibiting them from making the claim. Lizzy found it interesting that prayers had been removed from schools as far back as the twentieth century. They soon prohibited the mention of God or Jesus Christ in public. Her dad had told her how they reprinted all the money, taking 'In God We Trust,' off.

Of course that was when they had paper money and coins. Now everything was automated. One of the reasons there were so many unhappy people was the fact that with the automation came a lack of privacy. People felt that their every move was being watched. Smaller countries felt they were at the mercy of the larger countries of the world and this added to the unrest. She returned her attention to what she was reading.

"And ye shall hear of wars and rumors of wars: See that ye be not troubled for all these things must come to pass, but the end is not yet."

Lizzy looked up and stared out into the space around her. Those wars and rumors of wars had been going on for centuries. She read on.

"For nation shall rise against nation, and kingdom against kingdom; and there shall be famines, and pestilences, and earthquakes, in diverse places."

Surely she had been raised in a world of woes. There was constant bickering and battles between many of the countries of the world. She remembered the people who were killed when a part of California slid into the Pacific Ocean when she just a little girl. There were all kinds of people trying to bring food to the survivors. The Middle East was hit hard by one earthquake after another. Lizzy kept reading, but her reading was interrupted by the voice of John on the radio.

"Lizzy what are you doing?" he asked as his image flashed on the screen in front of her. She explained about the Bible she had kept as a family heirloom.

"I just felt the need to escape," she said softly. "I was reading of some of the predictions of Jesus." She looked into the monitor to see what kind of response she was getting. She wasn't even supposed to say his name. John was smiling.

"What are they?" enquired Adam as his image came on the screen next to John.

Lizzy explained about the wars and the earthquakes. Then she mentioned that Jesus said they were only the beginning of sorrows.

The men listened quietly. Neither of them had anything to say. At this moment they were predisposed to believe there was someone, anyone who had the power to help. Lizzy read aloud to the crews of all three shuttles. At one point she paused before continuing.

"For as the lightning cometh out of the east, and shineth even unto the west, so shall also the coming of the Son of man be. For wheresoever the carcass is, there will the eagles be gathered together. Immediately after the tribulation of those days shall the sun be darkened, and the moon shall not give her light, and the stars shall fall from heaven and the powers of the heavens shall be shaken."

As she laid the book aside, Lizzy took a deep breath.

"Wow!" She groaned. "Then we would have no place to hide." She found herself looking back. The sun was still there. The Earth was still there though there was no communication. She took comfort in that fact.

Lizzy backed up and read a portion that she had simply glossed over but suddenly felt compelled to read it again.

"For then shall be great tribulation, such as was not since the beginning of the world to this time, no, nor ever shall be. And except those days should be shortened, there should no flesh be saved: but for the elect's sake those days shall be shortened."

Lizzy spent quite some time deliberating what all this was supposed to mean. She realized that man had written all this off as superstition, but now she was searching for answers. She no longer was taking man's word for anything. She wanted to know how the universe came into being and she wanted to know if this God could actually take so many lives. Of course, she was not sure that any lives had been taken. Maybe this was simply an electronic failure of some kind.

John and Adam almost simultaneously broke her thought as they inquired what she was thinking.

They had watched her stare at the Bible in her hands on the monitor, but she had stopped reading.

She looked from one monitor to the other and then returned her gaze to the Bible before taking a deep breath and speaking.

"I think the Earth is in trouble," she announced. "We have spent centuries, now deciding that God was a figment of someone's imagination. We believe in nothing. That only leads to violence, selfish pride and devastation."

"Let's get some sleep," said Adam. "We'll wait till we get to the space station and see what is there. Then we will see if we can establish communications with the Earth again."

It made sense to him and John agreed. They signed off for some rest. Lizzy couldn't sleep, though. She had many questions on her mind. The biggest question was why did she feel that they were somehow doomed? That feeling would not last long.

Everyone else was asleep. While Lizzy was wrestling with this problem, suddenly, there was a man sitting by her side.

"How did you get here?" she asked.

"You've been reading the Bible," said Arty. "I am an angel of the Lord. I came to help give you peace."

"When did you get here?" Lizzy asked. Arty explained that he had been there all along. He told her he simply was waiting for a time when he could talk with her alone.

"You've been here all along?" she asked with some skepticism.

"Oh yes," said Arty. "Don't you find it interesting that after all these years you find yourself reading the Bible? People on Earth had decided several centuries ago that it was a fairy tale. Now, you find yourself in trouble, so you are searching.

"Is that a bad thing?" Lizzy asked.

"No. The fact is it is a good thing. Right now on the planet Earth there are a lot of people doing the same. This is their last chance for redemption. The Earth will be destroyed soon," Arty announced with a bit of sorrow in his voice.

"If you are an angel, why can't you stop its destruction?" Lizzy inquired.

"That's not my call," said Arty. "The Master already set things in motion. The fact is I am required by the Master to not go near the planet Earth, from this point in time until the Son of God comes. In the meantime, many will realize how far they have fallen from the Lord and be saved. Many others will find death."

Lizzy wanted to know why, but she didn't know how to put her questions into words. She knew in her heart that she had not been happy on Earth. She also knew now that someone had been calling to her, and that was what inspired her to become an astronaut. She simply didn't who was calling or why. Suddenly she understood.

"The great tribulation has come to Earth, hasn't it?" she asked. Arty nodded.

"Do Angels have names?" asked Lizzy. Arty nodded again.

"What's your name?" she pressed.

"Arty," he answered. He grinned widely when she started to laugh. Then he began to laugh, too.

"Do you find my name funny?" he asked.

"I would have thought it would be something like Gabriel," Lizzy chuckled.

"Gabriel was with the Lord from the very beginning, along with the Son. I was converted after spending some time in what you might call purgatory," Arty explained.

He then went into great detail of how he had been a bank robber who got killed trying to make a getaway in the old west, and how he and Andorra had been captives of Satan for a time until Harmony, another Angel of God had come to their rescue.

"A bank robber, becoming an angel!" Lizzy said incredulously. "That does not exactly sound like Angels.

"If you read the New Testament you will find that the Apostle Paul was someone who killed the new Christians. He met with Jesus on the road to Damascus and became one of God's own. God forgives whoever he decides to forgive," Arty informed her. "I guess I was one of those on whom he took pity. I didn't deserve it but he paid the price for my sins and now here I am. What's better, you will become one of us soon. Trust in God and keep reading that Bible," he instructed.

Lizzy looked down at the Bible that was placed in a set of brackets to keep it from floating about in the shuttle.

"I don't think I understand," she said.

"You will," Arty answered and faded away. When she looked up again he was gone. Lizzy lay deliberating for a long time before she finally went to sleep.

When she awoke it was as if she had dreamed the whole thing; however she felt God's presence and that made her feel comfortable.

Chapter 18 (Love Abounds)

Meanwhile, in the twentieth century things were heating up for Ed Wingert. He was listening to the voice mail left by Bee.

"I think she wants to see me," he sighed. Ed had not allowed himself to care about anybody until now. He had been with women but he would not consider marriage or even a romance with them. Bee was challenging him. It was not because she was the spittin' image of Audrey. He had always though Audrey was beautiful, although he never fell in love with her. Jack did that. Now he was having feelings about Beatrice which he was not in control of and it sort of scared him. He picked up the phone and called her. After several rings Bee picked up on the other end.

"Hello," she announced herself.

"Hi," said Ed. He suddenly was aware that he knew not what to say. She simply said she needed to talk to him. He knew she was troubled over the loss of her sister, and he did not know what he could say to comfort her. A long silent pause was the result of all these thoughts, as she stood completely tongue-tied with her phone to her ear. Finally Ed broke the silence.

"You wanted to talk to me," he began. "I think I need someone to talk to, myself. I was wondering if you would have dinner with me this evening."

It was only after he said it that Ed realized what he was saying. He was rather surprised because he had not intended to ask her out for dinner. He was even more surprised when she accepted. There was another thirty seconds of silence and then Ed spoke again.

"Can I pick you up at seven?" he asked. Bee accepted and, upon request, gave him her address. Then they both said goodbye and both simultaneously headed for the shower.

At six-fifty-five, Ed rang the doorbell at Bee's apartment. After he announced himself over the intercom she unlocked the door and he entered.

This was the first of many dinners they had together. At first they were both self-conscious, so the dialogue was mainly small talk, but as they became more familiar with one another, they began to see that they shared a lot in common.

During dinner one night Ed just blurted something out that he immediately regretted. but not for long.

"You know I saw Jack after the funeral," he said. "He came to me at my apartment." Ed looked into Bee's eyes, trying to ascertain what she was thinking of this wild idea but he didn't find shock. He found her to be extremely interested. Still he felt he needed to explain. He didn't want her to think he was crazy.

He explained the whole visit to her. When she didn't cut him off or act like she was becoming distant to him, he continued. When he finished, she shared news of her visit with Audrey.

"People would probably think we were crazy," she said. "I am sure she was there that night and I have felt her presence or someone like her ever since. You know, I've never been the religious kind, but I am starting to believe that God does exist and he is working in our lives. I think he has brought you to me. I thank him for that."

Jack reached across the table and put his hand on hers. His smile said more than any words he may have tried to say. Somehow right now, there were no words except

"I love you!"

"I love you, too," Bee answered. "I never thought I would love any man; you have been a source of real comfort," she continued.

"I guess we have comforted each other," Jack answered.

The next day, Jack didn't meet Bee for lunch as usual. He drove out to the prison to see how Joe was doing.

He went through the ritual as usual. He checked his keys and anything metallic in a locker supplied by the prison, walked through the metal detector and then waited until he heard Joe's name called out over the intercom. Then he got up and walked through the security gates that seemed to take forever to slide open and close behind him. He had, as usual, had a stamp on the back of his hand which only could be seen when he slipped his hand under the black light. Then he saw Joe who was in the general population now. He was sitting on a bench-like chair waiting.

Ed couldn't help but notice the smile on his face. Ed apologized for not coming back to see him sooner and Joe waved it off.

"I'm always glad to see you," he said.

During the course of their conversation, Ed asked how he was holding up and Joe surprised him.

"I found Jesus in here," he said as a matter of fact. "I have made some real friends. You know there are a lot of guys in here who swear they were framed.

Ed chuckled and asked if Joe believed them.

"No," Joe answered. "There are a lot of guys here like me," he continued. "They know what they did was wrong and now they simply want to pay their dues. A few of them will probably get paroled. I don't expect I will. I don't think I deserve it. But the fact is that no matter where I am, I know for the first time in my life that God really does have a place for me and I am going to live for him. I've kinda started a ministry in here. I want to help as many of these guys who will allow me to find where they are in life and build a future, if not in this life then in the next."

"You've come a long way," praised Ed. "I am glad you have found yourself. I believe in God, too. He has sent an angel to me. She's loving and she never misses a chance to praise me. I think I'm going to ask her to marry me." He was grinning from ear to ear and Ron smiled broadly.

"That's great," he said. "Remember to never stop loving her. Don't ever make her feel like she's second best and whatever you do treat her with kindness. I wish I could only do that with Sarah, now."

The rest of their visit was more small talk and before he knew it Ed felt the hand of a guard on his shoulder telling him his time was up. He said goodbye to his friend and left.

True to his word, Ed did ask Bee to marry him and she said yes. They were married about a month later and about fourteen months after that he came home from work one night to a glowing wife. Bee had an announcement to make. She was with child.

Their little baby girl was born healthy and Ed was feeling better about life than he had ever felt before.

Years flowed by. For Ed and Bee and their daughter, Mary Jane, it seemed to go too fast, at least for Ed and Bee. Mary Jane was the light of their lives.

For Joe things were going well, too, at least as well as you can expect for a man in prison. He had become an influence on the lives of many others who might have been career criminals, but instead found that life had much to offer for those who had faith. He watched many of them as they came up for parole, and he was never lonely because, like Ed, these guys did not forget a friend who supported them. They came back to visit on a regular basis.

Ed's life was about to take a change. Mary Jane was just seven years old and in school and Bee had taken a job as a library assistant to help keep the finances strong so they would be able to have a college fund set up for their daughter.

She noticed that one case Ed was working on was troubling him, but he wouldn't talk about it. She never pressed.

Then one day he came home from work with eyes glazed over. He shuffled through the front door and sat down at the kitchen table, saying nothing.

"What's wrong?" asked Bee.

"I killed a seventeen year old boy today," he groaned. "I didn't want to. It was him or me."

"What happened, Dear?" Bee asked, laying a hand on his shoulder.

"Actually, all I was trying to do was wrestle the gun away from him. He was threatening to kill people. I saw an opportunity and jumped for the gun but he stepped backward and we scuffled over the gun. It went off and he fell to the floor," Ed cried.

"In the Twenty plus years I've been on the force, I had never been forced to cause the death of another," he said.

"Now he's dead." Ed looked into Bee's eyes as if he were trying to gain some feeling of forgiveness. Actually that was all she had to give him. She knew nothing about the case and she did not understand how any of this happened.

Bee drew him into her arms. Ed said nothing for a long time. Then Mary Jane came into the room. When she saw her father with tears in his eyes, she began to cry.

"What's wrong, Daddy?" she asked. Ed pulled her to him and kissed her cheek. He didn't say anything. He didn't know how to tell his daughter what he had told Bee.

Later that evening he announced that he was retiring from the police force.

"I have enough time to earn a good retirement," he said. "I think I will try something else."

Bee didn't try to change his mind. In truth, she was relieved that he had made that decision. She had always been concerned that he may not come home some evening, leaving her and Mary Jane to live alone. After what had just happened, she was more acutely aware that it could have been him who received that bullet.

The next day, Ed turned in his resignation. Then later he stopped by to visit with Joe.

When Ed told him what had happened Joe gave the same exclamation that he so often used.

"Bummer," he declared. Ed went on to explain that he had turned in his papers. Joe asked what he was going to do and Ed said that he simply didn't know

"Look man," Joe began. "I found comfort in the Lord and my transgressions were a lot worse than yours. Maybe you should look to him, too."

Ed simply looked at him for a spell. Then he took a deep breath.

"I have prayed everyday that something like that would never happen. I guess he wasn't listening," he complained.

"He was listening," corrected Joe. "You need to keep in mind that everything, both good and bad will work for the good of those who love the Lord. You know what?" he went on. "You should consider becoming a minister. You could use your heartbreak as a tool. You know grief. You know what it does to you. You could help others out of the same pain. It would also help you out of your pain. It worked for me."

It wasn't long after that visit that Ed joined a seminary.

The years go by faster than anyone wants them to. Ed did become an ordained minister. He eventually got a job as a prison chaplain. He and Joe were always friends and Bee kept working as a library assistant. Before they knew it Mary Jane had grown up, fallen in love, married, and Ed and Bee were grandparents.

It was about thirty years after Ed graduated from seminary that his faith was put to the greatest test. Bee was diagnosed with cancer and there was no cure. He lost her but he knew she was with God.

It was only seven years after that when Ed got a visitor. He was going over some papers at his desk in the den at home when Arty came for him.

"You've done well," Arty praised. "Now it's time you come with me."

"Where too?" asked Ed, though deep down inside he knew.

"We are going to hook up with your wife," he smiled. "You're going to meet your Master."

"What about Mary Jane?" Ed asked. Arty simply reassured him that she was taken care of and it was Mary Jane who found Ed slumped over his desk. She had been raised to believe in God, so in spite of her sadness she knew her father was in his arms.

Joe, who did spend the rest of his life in prison, got the same visitor. Arty announced that the Master had forgiven all his transgressions and wished his company. He was found by a guard and that ended a saga.

Chapter 19 (What on Earth is Going On?)

Lizzy, John and Adam and their crewmembers were coming close to the space station and everyone was tense. They spent a lot of time with electronic equipment, trying to activate the communication equipment by remote control that seemed to be locked.

Lizzy worked along but her mind kept racing back to her visit with Arty. She also was curious about some books she had read long ago.

These were written by authors, many of whom simply disappeared or were thrown in jail as traitors.

One book especially was poignant to Lizzy now. It was a book called "Can Peace Exist?"

The book had questioned the forming of the World Council. According to the author it was formed in the late twenty-first century. At one point in history, according to him, the United States of America was the country that the rest of the world either hated or admired with all their hearts. Both respected their capabilities so that made them the leaders.

Somewhere along the way, the U.S. lost is leadership qualities and many of the other countries of the world pushed for a united organization. They had what they called the United Nations, although many thought it lacked power so they moved for something that would be the final word of law for the whole world. After many years of argument they came up with a government which every country in the world would have to answer to. This was a kind of demotion for the U.S., according to the author.

His book had gone on to mention that the World Council seemed to work for a while until countries in the Middle East decided this was not in their best interest to promote the council. It seemed to be for religious reasons that these countries were fighting many of the laws. One of these laws was that it was now against the law to practice one's faith in a God of any kind in public. He had written that this did not bother the people of America because they were slowly falling away from faith in God, anyway. Those Middle East countries would not give up theirs.

The author explained that terrorists had always been around but during the twentieth and twenty-first centuries they became more of a threat.

He was predicting an all out war before the century ended. He missed on the timing, but now Lizzy was wondering if that all-out war was not what was going on now.

Her train of thought was broken by a transmission from Adam. He was announcing that they would be docking with the space station in five minutes.

"Let's get ready to go inside as soon as we get there," he instructed. "Better have full suit and oxygen. We don't know what we're going to find."

He did not say this, but he did not expect to find anyone alive. After all, if there was anybody alive,they would have surely let them know by now.

The three doors opened almost simultaneously and people from the shuttles came through to see a horrible sight.

There were bodies floating around. Several of the crewmembers were doctors and they immediately instructed the others to help strap the bodies one by one onto gurneys which were meant to be slept on.

Now, came the unhappy job of trying to figure out why all these people died. The oxygen meter flashed its green light which let them know that there was plenty of oxygen in the space station. However, Adam instructed them to keep their suits on until they could find if there were any bacteria or viruses in the air which could be lethal to them.

"After all," he explained, "something killed these people."

For what seemed to be an awfully long time, the medical people searched for some reason for the death of the people on board. No bacteria or virus of any kind was found, so they reluctantly shut down their oxygen supply and took off the bulky space suits they were wearing.

Eventually, Dr. Eves came up to John with his preliminary report. It wasn't much. It was simply to explain that they could not figure why these people had died.

"They all died at about the same time as far as we can tell, but that is purely conjecture since their bodies should be rotten by now. There should be a horrible smell in here, but their bodies are fresh like they died today," Eves reported.

This was a strange situation. John, Adam and Lizzy discussed the possibility that they had been alive for a lot longer than anyone thought and that raised a question as to why they did not answer the calls that had been coming from Earth and more recently from their individual shuttles if they were still alive.

"One more thing," added Dr. Eves. "We have ruled out heart attacks. The post mortem showed no signs of an enlarged heart or even hypertension."

The doctor was at a loss to explain why they couldn't determine the deaths of these people. There had been no deaths classified as natural causes since the twenty-first century. Medical science had been able to find physical problems before they caused death and when a death did occur they had the knowledge and tools to find the reason. This time their wonderful technology was failing them.

They kept searching, hoping to find something they had previously overlooked. They ran tests on the people's kidneys, liver, brains and in the men, even their prostrate without having any luck.

Lizzy sat down in the pilot's chair and opened her Bible. She found herself reading it more and more. She remembered her father warning her never to let anyone know she even had that book. It was considered illegal reading since the late twenty-first Century. Somehow, she didn't think it would matter much now. As far as she knew, the Earth was gone.

She opened the Bible. Lizzy sat for a long time reading over the scriptures she had been reading before the shuttles docked with the space station. She found herself contemplating. She couldn't understand why she was drawn to the reading of the Bible which most people had declared as fairy-tale reading centuries ago.

"If there is a god," she thought to herself. "Why are we on a space station full of dead bodies with reason for being dead? Why was he not looking after them?"

None- the-less, she found herself reading and searching. She picked up on the following scriptures.

"Then shall they deliver you up to be afflicted, and shall kill you: and ye shall be hated of all nations for my name's sake. And many false prophets shall rise, and shall deceive many. And because iniquity shall abound, the love of many shall wax cold."

Lizzy was staring at the page without reading now. She knew of stories told by her father and his father before him of why religion was made illegal. There were many people who called themselves preachers of the word, who in truth were using the gospel as a way to make themselves rich.

"In short," her father had said. "They were selling eternal life to anyone who was fool enough to think he could buy it." He was constantly warning Lizzy to keep these things to herself lest someone want to harm her or have her arrested as a heretic. She wondered now if she should not have been yelling it to the mountain tops.

Adam came in just then. When he saw she was reading the Bible he said softly,

"You know, I think people were happier when they believed that." Lizzy smiled. She wasn't sure if he was lamenting the loss of truth or talking about loss of ignorance. Surely most people in this Century believed it was the latter.

"I think there may have been more to this Jesus fella than we thought," Adam continued. "I think maybe his predictions were not so far fetched as we wanted to believe. After all, we don't know what has happened on Earth, but there's something deadly wrong down there.

"Yes, you're right," said John as he walked through the door. We need to worry about what we're going to do next. We have no place to go. We wouldn't have enough supplies or fuel to get back to Earth even if we knew there was anybody left there. I'm afraid we don't have much time left."

Lizzy looked from one to the other than she sighed.

"Call me crazy," she said. "But, I am going to pray."

With that she bowed her head. Then Lizzy saw a vision. She wasn't sure what it meant, but it gave her a feeling of tranquility.

What she saw was a man dressed in white reaching out his hand for her. At first she hid her face with her hands in fear, but eventually dropped her hands and looked back at the man. Suddenly, she was compelled to reach for him. He took her hand and led her into a beautiful blue sky. That was when she woke up.

"It was a dream," she almost moaned. "I didn't want it to end."

"Didn't want what to end?" asked John from the doorway. Lizzy gazed at him but she wasn't really looking at him. She was simply staring off past him.

"Oh, nothing," she uttered. John didn't pursue any more and Lizzy went about her business.

Everyone was exhausted. They had been trying to find out what had caused the deaths of Frank, George, Allison and others for the better part of the day. They were also trying to contact Earth without success. Adam finally advised that they all needed to get some sleep. Maybe when they awoke they would be able to find what kind of a situation this had become. They all turned in. Sleep was not a problem for any of them. They each dozed off very quickly.

Chapter 20 (The Plan of Action)

The next morning John was awake before either Lizzy or Adam. There were a few doctors up and still trying to figure why all the people on board the shuttle died at about the same time. For that matter, they were trying to ascertain that they did, in fact die at the same time. This was against everything in their

medical journals.

Adam let them work. He had something else on mind. He wanted to see

if the telescope was up and working. One shuttle which was the last addition to

the space station had carried a telescope which was a hundred times more

powerful than anything they had ever used before. Theoretically, they should be

able to see objects on Earth with it. Of course, that would depend upon the

amount of cloud cover on the Earth.

He wanted to see if the people back home had actually destroyed

themselves. He knew there was talk about a war before they took off for outer

space. He had figured at the time that it was simply idle threats to get the other

members of the World Council to see things their way. Now he was concerned.

Adam found it rather ironic that it took being cut off from the Earth to

make him take it seriously. But if there was no life left on Earth, they had nothing

to go back to.

To his disappointment, he could not fire up the telescope. He was not sure

how much he would see should he fire it up. The Earth's orbit was moving away

from Mars and the Space Station. They had rushed their take-off because they

wanted to find out what had happened aboard the station, but they had also been

able to take off while the Earth & Mars were nearing one another. The Earth

would not be close to Mars for about a year and a half.

John soon came in and fixed a cup of coffee for himself and ate a little bit

of breakfast. The two did not say much to each other. John was trying to figure out the trajectories of the Earth and Mars for a different reason than Adam. He wanted to go home, no matter what he may find there.

He was studying the charts which showed the pattern of revolution of each of the two planets.

Like Adam, he knew that they had just made it to the station while the two planets were nearing one another and that now the Earth and Mars were moving apart. He also knew that at one point the Earth and Mars would actually be on opposite sides of the sun. He read to refresh his memory.

"Adam," he called. Adam came over to his partner. Then John read aloud.

"Earth and Mars trajectories are as follows," he read. "The Earth completes one orbit around the Sun in one year or three hundred-sixty-five days. Mars completes one orbit in six hundred-eighty-seven days. The more rapid movement of the Earth causes it to come near Mars every seven hundred and eighty days. It will be a while before we can even think about going home."

"I'm not sure there is a home to go too," Adam interjected. "I think they have finally done it."

John would not hear it. He was insistent that everything was fine. This just simply had to be a communication blip. Adam didn't pursue the conversation any further. It was too painful, anyway.

Lizzy came in a short while later. She looked much more rested but she had a strange look on her face. When John asked her about it, she told him about her dream. Then they were all quiet.

While she drank her coffee, Lizzy walked over to the opposite side of the space station. She had a beautiful close-up view of the planet Mars.

From here she could see the many craters and naturally occurring channels. She was reminded of what she learned about the ancient beliefs about the red planet. The Egyptians had named the planet Her Descher, meaning the red one.

Even up until the twentieth century there were those who believed that there was or at least had been life on the planet Mars.

Some believed in little green men. However in the twenty-first century man had landed robots on the planet and realized that what they thought were man or creature-made canals were simply naturally formed canals.

It was in the early two hundred twenty-second century when man actually landed on Mars and found it to be a barren rock.

Actually, there had been a break in the exploration into outer space after the World Council took control. Someone finally got them to start thinking about the possibility of finding another planet somewhere that would sustain human life. It had become obvious that the population was outgrowing the Earth's capacity. Someone had thought that one way to cut down on the population, since they no longer had the death penalty, was to send those who were convicted of violent crimes to another planet. In fact, that is what they had planned for the space station when they realized there were no planets which were inhabitable in the solar system.

As she gazed at Mars up close, Lizzy understood why the information was finally realized that there was no sign of organic chemistry on the planet. The atmosphere was primarily carbon dioxide with small amounts of other gases. There was no oxygen.

She returned her attention to the Bible she had smuggled aboard. Lizzy was especially curious about one scripture that she had glossed over at first but found herself drawn back too.

It read, "When you therefore shall see the abomination of desolation, spoken of by Daniel the prophet, stand in the holy place, (whoso readeth this, let understand: Then let them which be in Judea flee into the mountains."

She didn't understand this and there were no teachers to help her. She knew they were spoken by the Christ, but centuries had gone past and much of the readings in these ancient writings were simply not written for people of her era.

While she wrestled with the lack of understanding about the scriptures, John and Adam were wrestling with how to get back to Earth.

They had ascertained the approximate time they would have to turn the space station around and motivate it in the direction of the point in space where the Earth would be nearest to where they were now. They didn't know what they would find ,but for different reasons, each of them had decided they had to find out.

After careful consideration, they had decided that going back in the shuttles which they came in would be fool-hearty. The Space Station, with the shuttles now a part of it, had solar power. Although the shuttles worked much the same way, they would not withhold the stress of the long trip back and there would not be enough oxygen. The shuttles, like the space station, created oxygen using a special invention of a scientist of the twenty-fourth century. The invention was needed when it became apparent that the Earth was in trouble from global warming, pollution and the lack of plant life. People were taking up more and more room and rain forests were extinct.

The geoscientist who invention the O-machine, as they called it was able to use the same force that enabled plants and multicellular creatures like man to exist. The Sun was the beginning of it all.

The O-machine was able to create microbes. These are small but there are so many of them that they generate half the oxygen in the air on earth. They generate all the air the men onboard the space station breathed.

The space station had solar panels everywhere pointed directly at the sun. Although the suns rays were not as strong on Mars which was millions of miles further away than the Earth it still gave enough energy to create oxygen and power the ship.

Across the top of the living area of the space station was an artificial garden which used the carbon dioxide that the Astronauts breathed and that which was created by a special generator to feed a garden from which they were able to get food. Because there were so many people on board it seemed smarter to turn the space station toward the Earth and save the shuttles for when they got closer. That of course, was if there was anything left to get back too.

It was then that Lizzy came running in on the two men in a panic. She had just seen a flash of light which spooked her.

Then they all turned to look at the screen which showed images from a camera outside the station which was pointed toward Earth. It would not work earlier. John had tried to pull up the telescope through the screen without success but it was working now.

What they saw caused them all to gasp. The flash came again. It was a series of meteors. When they looked past them they saw a bright flash coming from where they believed the Earth to be.

Then they saw a bright ball of fire coming in their direction. Adam turned toward the pilot's cockpit.

"We gotta get this thing out of here," he yelled. "Posts everyone. Brace yourselves for impact."

It did not take long for Adam to realize that the space station was too big to maneuver quickly enough to get out of the way of the burning fragment that was heading their way. He opened the sound system and ordered everyone back to their shuttles.

John was concerned about this. He knew the shuttles did not create oxygen as fast as the space station and he knew there was no way to grow food onboard the shuttles. When he conveyed these concerns to Adam, he got a short reply.

"We don't have a choice," Adam practically yelled. "That thing is coming this way. It would take a miracle to get this thing out of orbit around Mars and even when we did, we would never be able to outrun that thing. It's heading right for us."

Everyone hurried for the shuttles and they all took off to move themselves out of the path of the oncoming fireball.

Chapter 21 (The Angels Multitask)

While all this was going on, the Angels had kept a low profile, per the Master's orders. The astronauts had no idea that the angels were there, but they watched from the shadows, although it was Harmony that kept Lizzy returning to the Bible.

Then they were called to the Master who had other jobs for each of them. He explained that they would keep a constant watch on the situation of the Space Station because what happened to the people who were now onboard the individual shuttles was of monumental importance.

At the same time, they had jobs to do in other points of time on the Earth. Arty was called to the old west to help a man who would father a son who would become a great inventor. It was the father's life that was in danger.

Harmony and Andorra had different jobs that were very much alike. Each was sent to help a young couple who were on the verge of breaking up. If this happened there were children who would not be born but who would play a part in creating things to come. The Master would not elaborate on what these great things were. The others were to simply wait in the shadows of space and watch what was happening to the three shuttles once they left the space station.

Both Harmony and Andorra were instructed to work undercover. The couples they were sent to help did not believe in Angels and the Master did not want them to know any differently at this time.

Harmony went about her task. Aiding her was Gabriel. At first, they simply stood in the heavenly shadows and watched.

Standing on the pier staring down at the rushing waters of the ocean was a middle-aged lady. She didn't show her age. One might have thought she was in her early twenties, but she was thirty-seven. Jane Louise was the mother of two. Her youngest was a girl of sixteen and her son was twenty-one. Actually he had just celebrated his birthday three weeks prior to this day.

Timothy or Tim was born when she was just sixteen. Her parents dealt with the frustration as well as they could. It seemed that in spite of their constant warnings, she and Andy were very much in love and could not stop themselves from enjoying the physical urge to make love. They had tried to be careful but were not careful enough because one day she realized that she had missed her period. At that time there were no tests to give instant reassurance of anything. But it was soon apparent that she was pregnant.

Andy did love her and he asked her to marry him and she accepted. Jane never got a chance to finish her education; Andy was already out of school and working as in a factory as a welder. The pay was enough for them to set up house and prepare for the bundle of joy that would soon be coming.

On the day of Tim's birth, Andy was showing every emotion possible from fear and panic to heavenly joy. Actually, Jane was simply scared.

The labor went on for what seemed to her an eternity, but it was rewarded with the loud cry of a healthy baby boy. Jane feared only her doubt about what kind of mother she could be. She soon realized that her heart would lead her, and motherhood was a reflexive thing.

For the first ten years of their lives together, they both were happy and totally devoted to one another. They had the greatest love for their children, too.

By the time Jane was pregnant with Judy, the husband was a part of the team. He went to classes with her and actually witnessed the birth of his daughter.

It was a short time after Judy's birth that Andy began to think about changing careers. He made good money as a welder but he wanted to do more.

After many discussions with Jane, Andy began school in the evening and soon had a degree in real estate.

The change was hard for both of them because even while he was in school Andy was working during the day and at school most every evening. That meant Jane and the kids had to work and play together without him.

Once Andy graduated from school, he went to work for a real estate firm. He seemed to be a natural at selling and money came in fast, although he was still spending too much time away from home. Jane found herself grumbling more and more about the man who was never there and the kids were not overly happy with the father who didn't have time for them, or the mother who seemed to take out her pent-up hostility on them.

The situation escalated. Because of her anger and his resentment of what he considered her lack of understanding, Andy found himself working longer hours than he actually needed. It meant more income for the family but it also meant more hard feeling between the two.

Their love life was dying a slow excruciating death. Their kids could see the chasm that was building but, had no idea how to help.

Andy soon found comfort in sharing his woes with his secretary. Yvette was a beautiful blonde lady who had never married and had always been rather in love with Andy. She would volunteer to stay late and help him with paperwork so they would have time to spend together.

Naturally, one thing lead to another and as far as Jane knew, Andy was going on a lot of sales seminars and other training vacations. What Jane did not know was that Yvette was going with him.

One of Jane's friends was on a business trip to Chicago during one of these seminars. Although she was not in real estate, she was staying in the same hotel with Andy and Yvette.

When she told Jane about the two kissing in a restaurant in Chicago, Jane went crazy. That evening when Andy came home, she flew into him like a wild bird. She called him a few names she had never used on anyone before.

"How could you?" she wailed. Andy tried to lie but he soon realized that the fact of the matter was that he was caught.

"What did you expect?" he soon screamed back. "All I get from you here is griping and complaining. When was the last time you actually rolled over in bed and actually touch me like you wanted me to make love to you?"

"I'm always asleep by the time you get in," Jane shouted back. "What am I supposed to do? You want me to cook and clean, take care of the children and still be in the mood for some consensual sex whenever you finally make yourself available?"

The argument went on, becoming louder and angrier and the children quietly crept away to their rooms.

"I'm through," Linda practically shrieked. "You ask your lover to move in and take care of the kids."

With that she stormed out of the house and walked. That was how she ended up on the pier this evening.

The ocean was going about its business without consideration for the woman standing on the pier. She stared at the waves as they washed ashore and subsided again toward the waves that followed, causing white foam to appear as the water swirled.

Jane found herself gazing at the horizon. The sea went on much farther than she could see and right now that only made her feel smaller than she already felt. She found herself wanting to jump. If she didn't die of the sudden impact with the water, she would surely drown and her sorrows would be over.

Jane leaned forward and began to climb the railing. That was when someone walked right into her causing her to cry out her frustration.

"What?" she yelled. "Are you trying to kill me?"

"Oh, I'm so sorry," Harmony apologized. "Are you alright?" In the shadows Gabriel was slightly amused. The woman wanted to kill herself and now she was angry at Harmony for almost pushing her off the pier. He understood that deep down, Jane did not want to die. She simply wanted the pain to end.

"I really am sorry," Harmony said again. "Sometimes I can be so clumsy."

"Oh, never mind," sighed Jane. "I was going to jump. Why am I mad at you?" She turned and looked at Harmony.

"Maybe I was really mad because you didn't hit me hard enough. If you had my troubles would be over."

Harmony smiled. She reached out and lay her hand on the hand of the beautiful lady as it rested on the railing.

"Why would you want to kill yourself?" she asked innocently. "Has life been that unfair to you?"

For the next half hour Harmony listened while Jane told her everything about her problems. When she had finished, Harmony gave her hand a motherly squeeze.

"You had your first child at sixteen?" she asked. "You didn't give yourself a chance to finish your own childhood. That is a shame, but ending your life can't help. Can you imagine how your children will feel if their mother commits suicide?"

Jane stared into the eyes of the lady who was speaking so softly and yet so loudly at the same time. What about her kids? She had not even given them a thought. What had they been thinking while she and Andy shouted obscenities at one another?

Now she really was exasperated. She couldn't just end her pain and leave them, but she didn't know what she would do. She could never forgive Andy. He had betrayed her.

Harmony stared at her. She then raised an eyebrow and asked her a question.

"What are you thinking?" she asked. Jane turned from the woman and stared into the ever moving waves again.

"I'm not sure," she answered. "I think I am simply numb. I thought Andy loved me, but I guess his secretary satisfies his needs better than I can."

"His secretary does not cook, clean and take care of two growing children," Harmony countered. "She could quite easily prove to be not as passionate about taking care of his kids. After all," she continued. "They are not hers. I have seen so many couples who have simply allowed themselves to lose touch with each other's feelings. The sad part is that each wants to blame the other when the blame, if there is any, falls on both."

Jane was still staring into the moving ocean while her mind was now trying to understand what this lady was saying.

Did she actually want Jane to blame herself for Andy's sin? Harmony knew her thoughts but went on talking as if she didn't.

"It isn't your fault that he fell. The question is, 'does he realize that his escape from reality was a mistake'."

In reality Harmony knew the fault, if you needed to place blame, is usually shared but she was not going to ask Jane to imagine this now.

Jane's mind was overwhelmed with too much pain and a feeling of guilt for walking out on her children like she did. She tried to put it into perspective, but the harder she tried the more things became overpowering to her. She leaned over the rail again. Harmony stood silent and made no move to stop her when she leaned even farther.

Suddenly she was plummeting off the boardwalk and falling into the water. Jane braced herself for the impact. To her surprise there was no pain as she entered the water. It was as if it were cleaning away all the pain she had been feeling. Jane knew this would bring death and she couldn't understand why she was not dead already.

Suddenly the water receded beneath her and she was lifted up to the boardwalk again.

She found herself staring into the ocean.

"Was that a body?" she thought to herself. Harmony answered her thought. She turned and looked into the Harmony's eyes as she heard her speak.

"That's your body," Harmony said.

"Right," exclaimed Jane sarcastically. "That's why I'm here looking down." She honestly wished she had jumped. She evidently imagined the whole thing.

"Reach out and touch the rail," advised Harmony. Jane looked at her with a quizzical look. At first she just looked. As she did so, her mind went about trying to understand what this lady was asking. It seemed to be a ridiculous request at a time like this. After a moment she reached for the rail and her hand went right through it.

Jane stepped back with a gasp. She tried again to touch the rail but could not. Then she turned toward Harmony. She said nothing, but the expression on her face was enough to let the angel know she had made her point.

"You know, taking the easy way out may seem to be the answer when you are in pain; I want you to see what it can do to those who love you.

With those words the ocean faded away and they were standing over an open grave. Jane knew the preacher. It was Pastor Johnson. Standing there with him was a group of her friends and relatives, including Andy and her children. The two were sobbing as they looked down at their mother's grave.

Jane didn't have words to describe what she was feeling. She shouldn't be feeling anything. She stood silently as the pastor said the words over her grave and then Jane watched quietly as everyone turned and slowly walked away.

It should not have surprising to her that her husband and children stayed behind. When Andy did take hold of their hand, Judy cried out. The words rang in Jane's ears.

"But, I want my mommy," the child wailed. Andy tried to be patient with her but he wasn't having much luck.

"This is only the beginning," said Harmony. "Judy is going to have a hard life without her mother."

"I will show you" said Harmony. She had no longer said that when the scene in front of them faded away and they found themselves standing in a darkened street.

"Where are we?" she asked, feeling her throat contract with fear.

"This," Harmony answered quietly, "is a street leading to where your daughter hoped she would find peace and happiness; it will lead to anything but."

A shady character came up to Judy, who was now seventeen years old. Somehow, she looked older around the eyes.

"You got the money?" he enquired. Judy reached into her purse and took out a wad of money and handed it to the man.

Harmony spoke quietly as she explained to Jane that Judy had sold the last piece of jewelry that had belonged to her mother to get Cocaine.

"Where's the snow?" she asked. The man pulled a plastic bag out of his jacket pocket and gave it to her.

"That should last a week or two," he said. "You've been snorting, right?" Judy nodded.

"You should try injecting," he advised. "It gives you a better high." Judy thanked him for the advice but said for now she would do what she knew.

"Why is she on drugs?" asked Jane. Harmony didn't answer. She knew that Jane already knew why. They would spend the next few hours or days following Judy as she reached for that euphoric feeling from the drug.

At some point Gabriel had slipped away, leaving this to Harmony. He needed to find what was happening with Andy.

Actually, he went back in time to the very moment that Jane went storming out of the house after their argument. The children were crying and Andy was beside himself with grief and guilt. He finally called his mother and told her the bad news. It wasn't long before Mom and Dad came in to look after the kids and Andy said he was going to look for Jane.

He didn't look for Jane, though. He headed for the local bar where he ordered a beer and sat staring at it for a long time.

After a while the bartender finished what he was doing with another customer. He could sense that Andy was in some kind of emotional stress.

"What's up?" he asked. Andy finally took a drink from the bottle. He simply shrugged.

It was at this point that Gabriel came in and ordered a beer. He decided to cut to the chase. Glancing over at Andy, he said hello. Andy simply shrugged again.

"You look like a man who has just lost his love," Gabriel said. Andy turned and looked him straight in the eye as if he were trying to figure how he knew about this. Gabriel saved him the trouble.

"I've seen it all too many times," he said flatly. "She walks out and he head for a bar. You ever hear that country music song, 'there's a tear in my beer'. "

"Yeah," Andy sighed. "I never liked it and I like it even less now." Gabriel took a sip from his glass.

"What happened? She find another lover?" he asked, though he already knew the answer.

"No," answered Andy. "I did." Then he opened up and started to share the whole story. Gabriel already knew but he listened as if he didn't. The bartender listened too.

When Andy was finished, it was the bartender who spoke. He drew another cold one for Andy and one for Gabriel, who had not even sipped from the first drink. As the bartender offered the drink, which he explained was on the house he said, "I know how easy it is for a man to slip and fall. I also know that it is hard for a woman to forgive someone when she has placed all her faith in a man and he falls. It's as if when he fell he dragged her along."

Gabriel listened intently as the bartender explained that he too had forgotten his marriage promises. Andy was just toying with his drink at this point. He wasn't even sure he wanted to drink.

"How can I ever make it right?" he asked. It may not have been a question as much as it was a statement, but the bartender answered.

"Find that woman and ask for her forgiveness," he said decisively. "She still loves you. She is just really hurt now. It will take some time, but you can still love one another."

This was when Gabriel spoke.

"You know something?" he asked and then proceeded without waiting for an answer. "Forgiveness is the most important part of love. You forgive her and she forgives you." He said nothing more. That left Andy staring into the almost full glass of beer.

"You need to find her, though. Who knows what she might do in a fit of despair. I know of one woman who took a header off a pier."

Andy looked from his drink to Gabriel. Then he jumped to his feet and headed for the door.

"Where are you going?" asked the bartender. Andy shouted back that he had to save his love and then went flying out the door.

Chapter 22 (The Plan for Eternity)

After the trip through time, Judy was disappointed in herself. How could she have been so tormented that she simply had not considered what her death would do to her kids.

"I should have never jumped off that pier," she moaned. Then everything went black. It was then that Judy heard Andy's voice calling from far away. The voice was getting louder and suddenly she opened her eyes and found herself lying on the pier with Andy caressing her face while he cried,

"Oh, baby, don't die on me." Judy jumped into a sitting position. Her first instinct was to look for Harmony, but she was not there.

"I thought I had lost you," wailed Andy. "Oh baby, can you ever forgive me? I should have shared my stress and concerns with you. I only know that I love you. I need you and I don't want to lose you. Please tell me you can forgive me."

As Andy helped her to her feet, Judy was still looking for Harmony. Finally she looked at the ocean below the pier.

"It was all a dream," she uttered. Thinking she meant his affair, Andy replied to her statement.

"I wish it were, but I was untrue to you. I promise I will never be untrue again," he said.

Judy stood looking into his eyes for a long time then nodded. He took her hand.

"Let's go home," he urged. Judy turned and walked with him. She did want to go home and hug her daughter and her son. From the shadows Harmony and Gabriel stood watching.

"That's one," breathed Harmony. Gabriel simply smiled.

Even as Harmony and Gabriel were working, Andorra was going about the task of helping a middle-aged couple who were in trouble. The problem was that neither Harvey nor Janet understood why their marriage was falling apart.

Janet was busy cleaning house in frenzy as Andorra knocked on the door, holding a Bible in her hand. Janet looked from her face to the Bible and started to close the door.

Andorra collapsed on the porch. The woman opened the door wide and rushed out to see if she was okay. She helped Andorra to her feet.

"Could I have a little water?" Andorra asked. "I think I am feeling a little faint." Janet sighed, silently nodded her head and led Andorra into the house where she drew a glass of ice water and proceeded to hand it to her.

"I'm sorry—I wasn't willing to talk to you," she said finally as she began to feel guilty over having almost slammed the door in Andorra's face.

"Oh, I get that all the time," Andorra said in a rather tired voice. "I take it you don't believe in the Bible?" she asked.

"I was raised in a church that taught me as much as I need," Janet exclaimed. "Of course, I thought I had heaven on Earth until now."

"Oh," proclaimed Andorra. "I didn't mean to upset you." Janet got herself a glass of water and sat down.

"Maybe it's a good thing to have someone to talk to," she said. "My mother thinks it's me." Andorra just listened quietly long after Janet had stopped talking. Then she took another drink from the glass.

"What's just you?" she asked. Janet began to explain what they had been experiencing.

Until a few months earlier there were no problems they couldn't tackle together, but then Harvey became moody, even angry sometimes. It could be about the least little thing. Things that never would bother him suddenly were becoming huge problems.

Janet had wanted him to go to a marriage counselor, but he refused, saying he didn't need some psychologist telling him how he should feel.

The two had three children—two boys and a girl—and they had always been the center of their lives. Harvey was suddenly always too tired to play games or go swimming with them. He didn't have any interest in her, either. He seemed to be pretty much self=possessed. They had even discussed the possibility of divorce.

After listening intently, Andorra took another swallow of water and asked Janet if that was what she really wanted. The answer was a resounding, "No."

"Every young couple goes through hard times," Andorra offered. "I tell you what. I am going to give you this Bible. When you really feel down, open it up and read. You may not believe in what you read, but you will gain comfort from it anyway."

Andorra lay the Bible on the table and excused herself. She quietly got up and walked out the door, leaving Janet there staring at the Bible. She would eventually open it and began to read the creation story. After reading for a while she felt tears filling her eyes. Janet tossed the book on the table. It did not close, but the pages turned and after drying her eyes, Janet picked up the Bible and began to read the 23rd Psalm.

Meanwhile, Andorra went after Harvey. She knew his problem. It was depression, but there was a physical reason for it. Andorra had to get him to a hospital. Harvey would not admit there was a problem so she could not simply advise him to go. She had to create a situation that would force him to go there.

When Andorra caught up with Harvey he was walking out of a bar. She thought fast. Andorra walked rather unsteadily as if she were drunk. As she got to where Harvey was walking, Andorra stepped in front of him and then wove out of the way again. She managed to lock a leg in front of his causing him to fall.

"Ouch," Harvey yelled as he fell to the sidewalk. "What's the matter with you, Lady?"

"Oh I'm sorry," Andorra apologized with a bit of a slur. "I guess I shouldn't have had that last drink."

As Harvey tried to get up he realized that he could not put his weight on his left ankle. Andorra acted as if she didn't notice and walked around the corner. She saw a police officer coming up behind Harvey as she disappeared.

"Are you alright, fella?" asked the officer. Harvey tried to stand up but the pain was enough to make him stumble. The police officer drove him to the hospital. Andorra was right there with him, though he had no idea.

Janet heard the phone ring. She climbed the stairs from the basement where she had been doing laundry, walked into the living room and reached across the Bible to pick up the receiver. She thought she felt something warm on her wrist as it hovered over the Bible.

"Hello," she answered.

As the doctor spoke, she found herself staring at that Bible as if it were glowing. She heard the words, but they didn't seem real and at the same they seemed to scorch her.

"Your husband was brought in with a badly sprained ankle," said Doctor Jackson. "You may want to come down here, Ma'am. There are some problems we need to consider."

"What problems?" Janet enquired. The doctor only explained that he would feel better telling her in person. When Janet asked if Harvey were alright she got an answer that was no answer at all.

"I hope so," said the doctor. "I'll be waiting for you."

Janet had to call a cab. Harvey had taken their only car. About forty-five minutes later she walked through the front door of the hospital. When she came to the information desk she gave them her husbands name and explained that Dr. Jackson was expecting her. They sent her to the doctor's office. This really struck Janet as weird. She would have expected them to take her to her husband. Now she was really worried that he had been sustained more than a sprained ankle.

As always, it took some time for the doctor to come in. Janet immediately asked if her husband was alright.

"The sprained ankle is not what worries us," Dr. Jackson began. While admitting him, we noticed his blood pressure was elevated. We took some standard blood tests just to be sure because a sprained ankle could cause some blood pressure elevation. We found his electrolytes were out of whack."

Janet swallowed hard but said nothing. She wasn't sure what to say, anyway. It seemed an eternity before the doctor started talking again, although it was only a couple of seconds.

"Has you husband complained with any uncomfortable pressure, fullness, squeezing or pain the center of his chest?" the doctor asked. Janet answered no to each.

"How about any pain, such as spreading to the shoulders, neck or arms?" he prompted. Janet shook her head.

"Has he shown any nervousness, anxiety or cold sweaty skin?" he continued to search.

Janet's eyes began to moisten. She remembered the arguments that usually started over trifles.

"Yes," she breathed. "He seemed harder to please and generally unhappy for quite some time now. I thought he just didn't love me anymore."

With this the doctor's questions became more demanding and for the forty-five minutes he was asking about things like Harvey's complete medical history. When it was over, he recommended that they give Harvey an ECG. He also wanted to check his cholesterol and keep Harvey in the hospital until they could do a complete run of tests.

"I fear Harvey may have had what we call a silent heart attack," said the doctor. "It may be a fortunate thing that he sprained that ankle. If we treat it in time we can help him

They did just that. It was two weeks later that the doctor prescribed a regimen of medicine for Harvey. He also recommended Harvey quit his job. Harvey's job was a high stress occupation and stress was just he did not need now.

It took some time, but Harvey soon was back at work. He found another job that was not stressful and he liked doing it. He learned how to work with computer software and worked with data.

Four years later, Janet gave birth to a son. This was what Andorra had to make sure would come to pass.

Chapter 23 (Back to the Future)

They all managed to survive the space debris which passed through, by maneuvering their vehicles out of the way of each meteor that came toward them. Then they breathed sighs of release all in unison.

What they didn't know was that back on Earth things were becoming extremely exciting, but for many horribly fearful.

A light came across the sky. At first it was hardly noticeable in the western hemisphere where it was daytime. In the eastern hemisphere where it was night people were awakened to find the sky glowing. Then people all across the world saw the image of the Son of God coming.

There was great fear on the part of many and wonderful joy on the part of others. Many bodies simply dropped to the ground. What those who were left behind could not see was the spirit of those people ascending upward toward the Son of God. Because of this their fear was even greater. They feared for their own lives.

Scientists had been predicting the deterioration of the Earth orbit around the sun for some time now. They were now fearful that the time had come. What's even worse, they now knew that Jesus Christ was real and they had fallen from their one chance at salvation.

One of those scientists was Abraham Monson. Aab, as his friends called him had written about it a long time ago. He had told how in the year 1972 scientists had noticed that the Earth had slowed down. They watched carefully until in 1999 they realized that the Earth was no longer lagging. They had all breathed sighs of relief and did not pay it any more mind. Aab had been saying that this slowdown could cause the Earth's orbit to deteriorate and thus move closer and closer to the sun which would make it uninhabitable to man.

Global warming had been a problem for quite some time so people had simply allowed themselves to become complacent. Aab had realized that without the automatic greenhouse that had been placed over the earth, the temperature would be much warmer than it had been a few hundred years ago. Nobody had taken notice because the giant air conditioner that kept things comfortable year-round did not allow the atmosphere to heat up.

Aab was called a heretic because he could see that the sun seemed to be bigger than the pictures from the past. There was one thing that even he was guilty of. He had lost faith in the Master early in his childhood.

Education is a good thing, but it must be learned along with the ability to realize that it does not explain everything. Aab had considered it to be his gospel. Shortly after the Son of God was seen, things really heated up. The system that kept the Earth so comfortable finally could not stand the increasing heat from the sun and it collapsed. At this point people were really in a panic as the heat almost instantly became unbearable. Within a few hours the oceans water heated up and it did not take long before they were hot enough to boil an egg.

Meanwhile the astronauts were still trying to get in touch with Earth. John began examining the radar and sonar equipment. He thought the meteor shower they had just experienced were parts of an exploded earth. When he finally did see what was going on he was not comforted.

"Adam, Lizzy," he shouted through the microphone. "I believe the Earth has been pulled into the sun." Adam was at a loss for words. He listened quietly. His mind was going in a thousand directions. Could this be true? His thoughts were interrupted by the sound of Lizzy's voice.

"John answered, saying unto *them* all, I indeed baptize you with water; but one mightier than

I cometh, the latchet of whose shoes I am not worthy to unloose: he shall baptize you with the Holy

Ghost and with fire: Whose fan *is* in his hand, and he will thoroughly purge his floor, and will

Gather the wheat into his garner; but the chaff he will burn with fire unquenchable," she said.

"Lizzy, what are you talking about?" inquired Adam.

"It's a verse from the Bible," explained Lizzy. "That is what's happening on Earth now. It's coming to pass."

There was silence for what seemed to be a long time. Nobody knew what to say. Most people on Earth had lost faith in anything in that book centuries ago. Now it seemed they should never have allowed themselves to be led astray.

"Lizzy, how did you get that book aboard?" asked Adam. "That should have been caught as contraband. Lizzy smiled silently. She had long before figured out that the new technology of the world was electronic. If it did not give out any electrical signals of any kind, nobody noticed. This was an old Bible that was written on paper with ink like they did in the old time. She was so happy now that her father had taken the chance and taught her to read. Nobody in this time read. Every book, every piece of information was recorded electronically and played on a device of some kind. Lizzy remembered her father warning her to never let anyone know she could read. This was something that had been outlawed a long time ago. Her mind took her back to the days when she thought her father was the most valiant of men. He dared to expand his mind when the whole world seemed intent on narrowing theirs.

She remembered her father telling her how he saved that Bible. He had allowed the inspectors to come and take away every piece of literature that was printed, but he would not let go of this wonderful document that meant so much to him. It had belonged to Lizzy's mother. She had died of cancer before they found the cure. He knew this Bible was her strength and now he would not let it be destroyed. He bundled it up in some insulation material and taped it to the top of one of the cold air ducts to the furnace. After the ozone machine went into affect they never needed a furnace, but most people never bothered to drag those old furnaces out of the house. They let them stay. Though heat was never needed, it did have a fan and an air filter, so it was not uncommon to keep the fan running. Scientists had perfected new electrostatic air filters that meant allergies were a thing of the past.

Lizzy reflected on something else, too. Her father had told her about snow. This was something she never experienced because it never got cold enough. For that matter, he had never experienced it either. The rain was created by the ozone machine and scheduled so it only rained at night and people were made aware of the schedule so they could plan around it. What's more, it never got too hot.

Lizzy was staring at the Bible but her thoughts were whirling around. It had to be extremely hot right now. The Earth was spinning into the sun.

This brought her mind back to the scripture she had quoted to the other astronauts. Her father had told her of the ancient writings that had at one time been revered, until man became too sophisticated to believe in such supernatural stuff. The irony was that it was all coming true.

Actually, according to her father, much of the predictions which people were still looking for in the twentieth century had already occurred during the lifetime of the original twelve apostles of Christ. Many of them had been put to death for their faith. This was one of the predictions of the Son of God. However, it was only the beginning.

Lizzy's Dad had often told her that he really thought the failure of the Christian religion was the fact that they allowed themselves to become split by different beliefs. Some read the scriptures which caused them to believe one thing, while others read the same scriptures which caused them to believe something else. The worse part was they let it cause them to hate one another.

"Hate," he would tell her over and over while she was growing up, "is a powerful and destructive passion. Somewhere along the way we all started leaning toward it and away from love. If only we had loved more, we might not be in the predicament we are in today."

Lizzy was called away from her thoughts as Adam sent a request to her through the radio. He simply wanted to make sure she was okay. He hadn't heard a word from her and began to worry. The request was just an excuse to break the silence without explanation.

"Can you tell me what that Bible you have tells us about what happens to us when we die?" he requested.

"As I read it," explained Lizzy, "it all depends upon the person and what's in his or her heart while alive."

Adam didn't press for more but he wasn't sure what that meant. People on Earth during this time in history did not consider what's in someone's heart. The only thing they knew about anyone's heart was the fact that it was the physical pump which distributed blood to the other body organs. For that matter, love, compassion and understanding were not considered to be quality traits. You looked out for yourself. Even the institute of marriage had become more a political thing than a sharing of life. Many husbands and wives did not see enough of each other to even get to know one another.

Adam almost got married once. It was arranged by his parents, and the parent of a girl he had grown up with. As he reflected back, he never really liked that girl, but if Mom and Dad said you will marry her, you did.

The week before the marriage, the girl was in an accident at work and died. The following month his Mom and Dad were in a house fire and died of smoke inhalation. So, Adam was unmarried and he was truthfully happy with that.

There was a long spell of silence as each of them contemplated what had happened on Earth and what would happen to them. They were certain they could not survive for a long period of time. The plan was that food and materials needed would be coming from Earth, but now there was no Earth.

While each reflected in his or her own way, Lizzy opened the old Bible again. This time she read from the beginning of Genesis.

"Thus the heavens and the earth were finished, and all the host of them. And on the seventh day God ended his work which he had made; and he rested on the seventh day from all his work which he had made," she read. "And God blessed the seventh day, and sanctified it: because that in it he had rested from all his work which God created and made.

"These *are* the generations of the heavens and of the earth when they were created, in the day that the LORD God made the earth and the heavens, And every plant of the field before it was in the earth, and every herb of the field before it grew: for the LORD God had not caused it to rain upon the earth, and *there was* not a man to till the ground. But there went up a mist from the earth, and watered the whole face of the ground. And the LORD God formed man *of* the dust of the ground, and breathed into his nostrils the breath of life; and man became a living soul. And the LORD God planted a garden eastward in Eden; and there he put the man whom he had formed. And out of the ground made the LORD God to grow every tree that is pleasant to the sight, and good for food; the tree of life also in the midst of the garden, and the tree of knowledge of good and evil. And a river went out of Eden to water the garden; and from thence it was parted, and became into four heads.

The name of the first *is* Pison: that *is* it which compasseth the whole land of Havilah, where *there is* gold; And the gold of that land *is* good: there *is* bdellium and the onyx stone. And the name of the second river *is* Gihon: the same *is* it that compasseth the whole land of Ethiopia. And the name of the third river *is* Hiddekel: that *is* it which goeth toward the east of Assyria. And the fourth river *is* Euphrates. And the LORD God took the man, and put him into the Garden of Eden to dress it and to keep it. And the LORD God commanded the man, saying, `of every tree of the garden thou mayest freely eat:  But of the tree of the knowledge of good and evil, thou shalt not eat of it: for in the day that thou eatest thereof thou shalt surely die. ` And the LORD God said, `*It is* not good that the man should be alone; I will make him a help meet for him. ` **And** out of the ground the LORD God formed every beast of the field and every fowl of the air; and brought *those* unto Adam to see what he would call them: and whatsoever Adam called every living creature, that *was* the name thereof.

 And Adam gave names to all cattle, and to the fowl of the air and to every beast of the field; but for Adam there was not found a help meet for him. And the LORD God caused a deep sleep to fall upon Adam, and he slept: and he took one of his ribs, and closed up the flesh instead thereof; And the rib, which the LORD God had taken from man, made him a woman, and brought her unto the man. And Adam said, `this *is* now bone of my bones, and flesh of my flesh: she shall be called Woman, because she was taken out of Man. ` Therefore shall a man leave his father and his mother, and shall cleave unto his wife: and they shall be one flesh. And they were both naked, the man and his wife, and were not ashamed."

"That sounds pretty heavy," said Adam. Only then did Lizzy realize that she had been reading aloud.

"The first man made by God according to the Bible was named Adam," she said. Adam didn't say anything for a long time. Then he broke the silence.

"What ever happened to your father?" he asked. Lizzy found her eyes becoming misty as she searched memories that she had tried hard to avoid until now.

While she tried to construct a conversation to explain as much as she knew to explain to Adam her mind was digging deep for something she could say.

It took her back to her teenage years.

Chapter 23 (The Heretic)

From the shadows, Arty was searching for some answers to help her with. He went back to the days of her teenage years. It was just like turning the page of a book to him. He knew he couldn't change anything and when he found the time slot he realized that Gabriel had already been working. He also realized there was a reason for her father's death. It was, in fact, his passage into eternal life.

There was her father sitting in front of a computer. It was much more than the type of technology that created the computers in the twentieth century, but it was by this time still an antique version. However the old man had set up a sophisticated firewall and was working feverishly to share some of the knowledge written in the age-old Bible he had—the one that went into space with his daughter years later. He knew he was taking a horrible chance because this was considered to be a capital offense. The Bible had been proclaimed as a form of brainwashing. The old man, John Jordan, thought the brainwashing was on the part of the World Council which had taken command of the whole earth. Whatever they proclaimed everyone abided by, even the government of the United States.

Lizzy remembered her father often saying that he believed that the United States simply grew too large to sustain its strength. He told her of many nations that had risen and fallen throughout the ages, including the Great Roman Empire. He would often remark that he remembered the scripture where Jesus Christ proclaimed that there would be wars and rumors of wars, and he never quite understood why people didn't realize that it was happening right under their noses.

One day Albert, who Lizzy still called Papa, decided to start telling people who were deprived of the holy word. He got an old computer which was outdated but cheap to buy, and knowing computers, he set up a program to mask his writings from anyone who did not have the software to open it. He didn't want the government to shut him down before he told people of the great wisdom they were being deprived of.

Before too long, he had a network of people around the globe who were curious at first but soon became regulars on his site. He had taken special precautions to set up a firewall and antivirus protection so nobody could get in without his approval. He felt that he was doing a service.

The unfortunate thing was that one of the visitors who had long since given up on any kind of faith turned him in.

It was a morning like any other when the gray haired man strolled into his office. His electronic secretary played off his messages from the phone. One of them was from the man who turned Albert in. The problem of getting in to check out the site was not hard. The man had sent a copy of the special software that Albert had created for those who were interested in his program. What Andrew Murphy was interested in was how many other people had this man reached.

Andrew called in several of his experts to see what could be done about this heretic. He was nervous because this was the kind of thing the World Council would not take lightly.

"Whoever this guy is, he is breaking the Council's laws," he told them. "The United States is having a hard enough time trying to maintain a prominent place on the Council. If the Council finds out about this man it won't help us at all."

He had his software experts create a worm that would easily be hidden in the old machine that was sending this stuff and then track down the IP addresses of each machine that was receiving it.

One by one, Albert noticed his following falling off. He thought they just didn't believe. What was really happening was what he had hoped would never happen. Officials of the World Council were arresting these heretics. They were not given trials. They simply disappeared.

Soon it would be Albert's turn. Once Andrew and his henchmen were certain that they had all his followers they came to take Albert.

All Lizzy knew was when she came to his house one night he was not there. She called the officials and went through the procedures that were regulated by the World Council; somehow she didn't feel like they were trying very hard.

It had been many years since then, but Lizzy had never really given up the hope that she would see her father again. She would never give up that Bible which she carried aboard the shuttle with her when she went into out space and now she was so glad she wouldn't let it go. Now the Earth was plummeting into the sun and would soon be no more. The simple fact was this. There was most likely no life left now. She wondered how long she and the others aboard the not finished shuttle would last before they were no more.

"Lizzy," called Adam. "We need to talk." Lizzy asked what they need to talk about. She was beginning to feel that things were pretty much hopeless.

"John brought up a good point. The others all agree. We need to pull our ships back together and dock. We can never survive in pieces.

"But the shuttle is damaged," protested Lizzy. "We can't possibly keep that thing going. We are all doomed." There was a really morbid sound to her voice as she said that.

"John was just saying that the oxygen machine is in the center of the main shuttle. It should not be damaged. We need to dock our ships and make a small version of the shuttle from them. Then we will go into the main shuttle to get the oxygen machine and other supplies that are still usable and install them in our smaller shuttle.

"As soon as we do that," responded Lizzy, "we will be hit by another meteor shower." John had already looked into that possibility. Using the radar equipment he had he found that there was nothing coming for millions of miles.

"Besides," Adam pointed out. "If that happens, we split again to ride it out and then redock."

The crew went about the task of doing what was needed to be done. The Angels stood silently and watched except for those constant trips into the past to help somebody who was in need
on the Earth. Adam and his crew went into the main part of the unfinished shuttle. They found an awful lot of damage which was done by the meteor storm. Adam reported to the others what he saw.

"It's a good thing we got out of here," he said over the radio. This place is leaking like a sieve. I only hope the oxygen machine hasn't burned itself out trying to produce oxygen from nothing."

His fear was relieved. The oxygen machine was still running and no damage was found. They took on the task of shutting it down, disassembling the machine, and carrying it back to Adam's ship. Once they all docked, they reassemble the oxygen machine and used it to produce enough oxygen for everyone aboard.

Nobody seemed to want to think about what would come next. Earth was gone and they would simply be suspended in faith for the rest of their lives. There was no plan of action because nobody knew what would come next.

Every opportunity Lizzy had, she pulled out the old Bible and read. One day while she sat staring at the book, Adam asked what was so intriguing about that book anyway. Lizzy looked up and smiled.

"It was my Dad's," she said. It also predicted the sort of thing that has happened would come to pass. Dad always said it would. Did you know the first man created according to the Bible was named Adam?"

"Oh, really," proclaimed Adam. "Was the first woman called Lizzy?
Lizzy smiled again.

"No, her name was Eve," she replied.

Adam began to sit with Lizzy while she read from the Bible. They discussed things and Lizzy was delighted that someone was interested enough to share the book.

One day while they were reading, John called for Adam.

"We have something coming," he almost screamed. "I don't know what it is but it's everywhere.

"Did you get a reading on the radar?" enquired Adam. John answered that nothing showed on the radar, but whatever it was it was massive.

"It's like the brightness of the sun," he proclaimed. "But it seems to have no mass. I mean there is nothing of any substance to it. It's just a huge light."

Everyone scrambled to see where they might go to get out of the way of this thing although they all knew evading it would be impossible.

"Maybe the thing will just pass through," said Adam. "Maybe it is just some sort of optical illusion. It doesn't show any kind of electrical or magnetic force. It doesn't show up as anything. It is only something we see."

"Maybe we're just going crazy," replied John. "We have been out here for almost two years."

They couldn't do anything but watch as it rushed toward them. Suddenly it was all around them and they felt something none of them could describe.   Then something even more unbelievable happened. The ship seemed to disappear and they were standing in the brightness. However, now the brightness did not seem so harsh. It became something beautiful. There was a numbness that they all felt. Lizzy thought it was just a rush of adrenalin, but Adam suddenly felt scared and reached for her. He could not touch her.

"What's happening to us?" he gasped. As he said that there was a rough looking cowboy walking out of the brightness which had become more like a mist. At first he looked dirty with a gray straggly beard and an old beat up hat, but as he stepped closer to them the hat became white and suddenly began to glow. The cowboy outfit also began to turn white. It soon turned to a robe of pure whiteness as did his hair and even his eyelashes.

"Hi," he introduced himself. "My name is Arty. We've been with you guys, watching over you. Now we are here to take you home."

"Home?" Adam repeated in the form of a question. "Our home has been destroyed."

"Oh, that was Earth. No, I mean your eternal home." He looked at Lizzy.

"I have noticed you've been reading the good book a lot. That's good. There is a lot of true knowledge in it." Then he turned his attention back to Adam and acknowledged all the rest.

"Your home," he began is Heaven. Follow me." Arty turned and walked through the brilliant mist. The astronauts simply followed.

Before long, they could see something shining through the mist. It was a beautiful color of gold. As they got closer they could make out what it was a pair of giant golden gates.

"These are the Gates of Heaven," said Arty. As he spoke the gates swung open and he began to walk through. Adam almost decided to turn and run the other way when he realized there was no place to run. Arty knew his thoughts.

"Don't be afraid," he encouraged. "We're heading into the most beautiful land that ever existed." Adam started walking.

Eventually the mist was gone and they saw a beautiful garden in full bloom with every kind of flower you could think of.

"They are in bloom constantly," Arty announced. "Come on, I want you to meet some friends.

Suddenly a host of individuals were standing with them. They were all dressed in white robes.

"Hi Lizzy," came a familiar voice. Lizzy turned and there stood her Dad. She wanted to hug him, but wasn't sure she could touch him. The fact was she was not sure she wasn't dreaming.

"This is no dream," said her father. "Ella, our daughter is here," he called in the same voice that would have used to call his wife out of the kitchen. Sure enough, there was Lizzy's mother.

Lizzy was not the only one to be reunited with lost loved ones. This was a wondrous day. After a long visitation Arty announced something.

"There is someone else you need to meet." He turned and looked off into garden and kneeled down as another man in white came walking along. The others took the hint and kneeled down, too.

"This is Jesus Christ," announced Arty. "He is the one who saved my soul and yours. He is here to explain why we are all here and what comes next.

With a voice so loud everyone could hear and yet so soft that it brought a wonderful feeling of peace to all, Jesus explained that they were the one-hundred and forty-four thousand who had been written about in the Bible. With the exception of Lizzy and Adam, nobody from their era had any understanding of what he was talking about but felt compelled to listen.

It was Adam who had a question he felt needed to be answered. He was nervous but he had to know. He felt this might be off the subject; everything that had happened had come to pass so quickly that he had no time to sort it out.

"What are we supposed to do here?" he asked with a puzzled, almost strained sound to his voice. "I mean, what can we accomplish by being here, anyway?"

"You are here for a briefing," answered the Son. "You will be sent back to Earth as Angels of the father to save as many souls as possible before it is too late."

"But the Earth is no more," Adam retorted. "The Earth is a thing of the past."

Jesus' smile was bright as he tried to explain something that Adam and for that matter any of those present had not thought of.

"Think of it this way, my brother," he began. "The Father always was. He had no beginning and he has no end. Yesterday, today and tomorrow are all the same to him. There is no past for he exists through all time."

"I don't understand," said Adam. "Either it was or is or is yet to come. That's what I understand."

"Think of it this way," offered the Son. "Consider a minute. Then consider a second. Now, break that second down to milliseconds. Keep going and eventually you can't even count it any more. God has been for eternity. Think of a minute in eternity. That minute, that second, that hour, day, or even year seems pretty small. Time to us is as another dimension to travel through. Yesterday, today and tomorrow are all the same. This brings us to your assignment. It is a job you derive great satisfaction from. You will learn about how mankind has evolved and you will visit each stage of that evolution. There are more souls to be saved and you will play a part."

Adam listened quietly as the Son explained the plan. They would go back to an Earth that Adam thought was no more, but during a time when it was thriving with life, and he would help people learn more about God and his will for mankind.

"At first," explained the Son. "You may simply take on the form of a homeless person in hopes that someone will find it in their hearts to help you. By doing so, they will have helped themselves."

"Some have entertained Angels unaware," breathed Lizzy. Jesus smiled. His eyes were soft with love and compassion.

As Adam took in the conversation, he also found his eyes roving to and fro. In the distance he saw his old friend George but only saw him as George for an instant before he realized that like everyone else he had been changed into a spirit so pure that nothing of his old friend was the same.

"Lord," he asked. "Why is God not here?" Jesus smiled with understanding as he raised his arms wide and high as if embracing the sky.

"The Father is here," he said. "The fact is that the father is in everything and in everyone. The very DNA that you are made up of is a part of God. He is in the Heavens and he is in the earth."

"I don't understand what you're talking about," said Adam. "How can he be everywhere at the same time?"

"First, time is only a dimension," explained Jesus. "To the father as with me, time is of little consequence."

"But you said we were going back to a world that no longer exists," Adam began. "That seems rather hard to do if it isn't there."

"I don't think you're getting the big picture," answered the Son of God. "Imagine having lived forever. No beginning and no ending. Imagine what a year or a day is like to someone who has always been and will always be. I once told my disciples before they hung me on that cross that a day is as a thousand years to the Lord. Think about it. If that were true seven days to God would be seven thousand years. One year would be three-fifty-six thousand years. Now if you want to pursue this multiply by a hundred years or a thousand years. If you look from another point of view, divide a day into hours or an hour into minutes. Go further than that. Divide the minutes into seconds or milliseconds. Keep going and you get to the point where the fragments are so small that you can't even measure them anymore. Time to God and time to me is simply another dimension through which to travel. As of now it is another dimension to you also. That is why you will be able to visit Earth during its various periods of evolution and help many who have not yet seen the Master but who deserve the opportunity. I hope this has answered your question."

"All of life and all of time is at my command," declared Adam as he realized the wonder of the gift he had received. He hadn't really meant to say it out loud, but the Son smiled and reassured him that this was so.

"There is one more thing to expand your vision of the Father," said Jesus. He is in every leaf that blooms on every tree every spring throughout all of eternity. He is the tree, the grass, the mountains, the sea, the thunderstorms, hurricanes, typhoons and gentle spring or summer breeze. He is every snow flake that falls in the winter and he is even in the heat of the sun. The fact is he is the sun. God is even the void in space where nothing exists."

There were many questions posed by others. Ed, for instance who had been reunited with Jack and Audrey, still could not understand how a loving God could allow the destruction of the Earth.

"The Earth, my friend, was on its way to its own destruction," Jesus answered. "There was a group of states within the World Council that had been secretly working on nuclear weapons to start what they called a revolution. Those bombs would have created more pain over a long period of time than those people endured. It breaks our hearts to see even one who is lost but the father cannot, will not go back on his word and he did give man free choice. I have a question for those of you who were astronauts. Why did you want so badly to explore space?"

"We wanted to find out what was out there," answered Lizzy. Jesus smiled at her and without a pause answered.

"You were still searching." He said. "In the twentieth century someone found out what caused illness. He said they were germs, viruses which cause high fevers and can cause a man to become delirious. He was right. Somehow though, this seemed to make my casting the demons out of Legion less of a miracle to many. Most doctors still believed but many became caught up in their education and quit asking more questions because they thought they had found all the answers. They stopped growing."

Jesus then began giving instructions to each of the Angels. Arty was never to take on the demeanor of a cowboy, Andorra could never be a bargirl again. After all, Mordrid was still alive and working for Satan in the time slots they would find themselves working. He could never know he had not succeeded in destroying them.

Ed, Jack and Audrey would use their earthly talents in a heavenly way to stop people from making the one mistake that would lead them to destruction.

"Not all of them will be success stories," warned the Son. "Some will ignore you and go their own selfish way. Save the ones who will follow."

Then Jesus dispersed them to their first assignments. On a clear and sunny day in the year 2009, a lady was driving her new hybrid car when she noticed an old lady in a wheel chair that seemed to be stuck in a storm drain. Her heart went out to the lady so she stopped to help Andorra. Little did she know she was helping an Angel of God.

This Story Has No End!

www.ingramcontent.com/pod-product-compliance
Lightning Source LLC
Chambersburg PA
CBHW020956180626
46814CB00003B/1111